BABY HELP

Other Titles in the

True-to-Life Series from Hamilton High

by Marilyn Reynolds:

Too Soon For Jeff

Detour for Emmy

Telling

Beyond Dreams

But What About Me?

BABY HELP

True-to-Life Series
from Hamilton High

By Marilyn Reynolds

Buena Park, California

Library of Congress Cataloging-in-Publication Data

Reynolds, Marilyn, 1935-
    Baby help / by Marilyn Reynolds.
        p.   cm. -- (True-to-life series from Hamilton High)
    Summary: Because her partner continues to abuse her,
seventeen-year-old Melissa takes their young child and goes
to a shelter for battered women where she begins the healing
process.
    ISBN 1-885356-26-9 (hc). -- ISBN 1-885356-27-7(pbk.)
    [1. Abused women--Fiction. 2. Family violence--Fiction.
3. Women's shelters--Fiction.]   I. Title. II. Series:
Reynolds, Marilyn. 1935-   True-to-life series from Hamilton
High.
PZ7. R3373Bab   1997
[Fic]--DC21   97-40246
                                                            CIP
                                                            AC

MORNING GLORY PRESS, INC.
6595 San Haroldo Way   Buena Park, CA 90620-3748
    (714) 828-1998   FAX (714) 828-2049
Printed and bound in the United States of America

Again I lift her from the crib. In my head I hear Rudy's furious scream of "Stop with that goddamned baby help crap!" and suddenly the white hot anger I've not felt for myself starts in my belly and moves through my body, filling me from head to toe with a fiery rage, clearing my brain, showing me the way.

I'm getting out of here. I'm getting Cheyenne out of here. Maybe he could break my spirit. Maybe I didn't have much spirit to begin with. But he won't break Cheyenne.

Like Marilyn Reynolds' other novels,
Baby Help is part
of the **True-to-Life Series from Hamilton High.**
Hamilton High is a fictional, urban, ethnically mixed
high school somewhere in Southern California.
Characters in the stories are imaginary
and do not represent specific people or places.

ACKNOWLEDGMENTS

I wish to thank:

Barry Barmore, Karen Kasaba, Michael Reynolds and Anne Scott, for offering critical insights and general encouragement.

Donna Marie, of the YWCA-WINGS program, for her expert advice and generosity of spirit.

The Farris family, for providing a quiet writing retreat when it was most needed.

The movers and shakers of Morning Glory Press.

Dianna Perez and Jennifer Avila, Century High School readers who offered helpful comments along the way.

Students at Reid High School in Long Beach, and in the Fullerton Joint Union High School District, who expressed interest in a continuation of the original "Baby Help" story.

Ashley Nicole DiFalco Foncannon, for providing the original model "baby helper."

Subei Reynolds Kyle for providing the quintessential two-year-old model at just the right time.

Marilyn Reynolds

Dear Readers,

*The road to breaking free of an abusive relationship is usually long and complex. I started Melissa Fisher on that road in the short story, "Baby Help," which is included in **Beyond Dreams,** a collection of short stories in the True-to-Life Series from Hamilton High. But it was clear to me that the short story was only a beginning, and that Melissa's road would have more twists and turns than a mere twenty-four pages could chart . . . hence **Baby Help,** the novel.*

Marilyn Reynolds

To Subei Reynolds Kyle

1

In my Peer Counseling class today we have a guest speaker from the Hamilton Heights Rape Hotline. I'm sitting in the back of the room, pretending to take notes, but really I'm writing my name over and over again, as it is, and as it will be. Melissa Anne Fisher, Melissa Anne Whitman, Mrs. Rudy Whitman.

Melissa Fisher has thirteen letters in it. I think I've had a bad luck name. If my name changes to Melissa Whitman, with fourteen letters, maybe my luck will change. I think it will. I touch the bruise on my upper arm, lightly, through the sleeve of my long-sleeved blouse. Things will be different when my name changes.

Rudy and I have been together for three years now and, next to our baby, Cheyenne, he's the most important person in my whole life. And I'm important to him, too. Before Rudy and Cheyenne, I wasn't important to anyone but me, and that wasn't enough. Rudy has his faults. I'm not saying he's perfect. But nobody's perfect. Right?

At the front of the classroom the guest speaker is writing her name on the chalkboard. Paula Johnson. She says to call her Paula. She looks young enough to be a student here at Hamilton High School, but Ms. Woods introduced her as a college graduate with a degree in social work.

"Let's define rape," Paula says, turning to face the class.

"Being forced to have sex when you don't want it," Leticia says.

"Right," Paula says. "How can someone force a person to have sex with them?"

"By overpowering them," Christy says.

"With a gun or a knife," Josh says.

Paula writes responses on the board, under types of force.

I write Cheyenne Maria Fisher, Cheyenne Maria Whitman, next to my own names, half listening to the talk about rape, half concentrating on the names in front of me. Cheyenne is two now. I love her most of all. Even more than Rudy. Even more than myself.

Last summer when we were practically dying of the heat, we went to Rudy's aunt's house, to use her pool. I asked Rudy to watch Cheyenne while I went in to the bathroom. I came back out just in time to see my baby fall into the deep end of the pool. I ran to that end, jumped in, grabbed her and held her over my head.

I can't swim, but I didn't even think about that. I just knew I had to get her out. I was swallowing water, holding her up, when I felt her lifted from my hands. I sank down, my lungs burning for air. Rudy jumped in and dragged me to the side and his uncle pulled me out. I lay there coughing and gasping for air, sick with all the water I'd taken in.

Rudy said I was stupid, that he saw her too and could have rescued her faster. But I didn't care — all I saw was that she needed help. Anytime my baby needs help, I'll be there, even if it means risking my own life. That's how I know I love her more than myself.

"What if the girl asks for it?" Tony says.

"What do you mean?" Paula asks.

"You know — like if a girl is a big tease and she gets the guy all horny and then she yells rape when he does what she's been asking for all along."

"So let's get this straight. The girl comes on to him, maybe she's wearing clothing that shows a lot of her body, and then he forces himself on her?"

"Well, yeah. But she asked for it."

"If any of you think that's okay, you've got a good chance of ending up in jail. Never is it okay, never is it legal, to force sex with anyone, young or old, male or female, friend or stranger. Never. She can take off all her clothes and strut her stuff right in front of you, but if she says no to sex, and you force yourself on her, you're committing rape."

Questions are flying around the room now. What if she says yes and you're already, like almost there, and then she says no? Can a girl ever rape a guy? What about if you've got these plans, like say after the prom is going to be the big night, and the guy rents a limo and takes her to a hotel and he's got condoms and everything because that's what they've planned, and then she changes her mind? What about if you're married?"

Paula writes the questions on the board as fast as she can. I write Rudy Charles Whitman on my paper. I write our names in a forward slant and a backward slant, dotting the i's with little hearts, getting my Flair pen out of my backpack and going over the ball-point writing to darken it. I like how the names look, and how Whitman looks after Cheyenne Marie, and after Melissa Anne. I like the feel of the W under my pen. It is a prettier capital letter than the capital F of the name I've always had.

I practice capital *W*'s while the buzz of discussion goes on around me.

"Anytime anyone touches you in a way that you don't like, that's abuse. It may be sexual abuse, or it may be physical abuse, but if you don't like it, and if you've made that known, and it continues, that's abuse."

"Are abuse and rape the same thing?" someone asks.

"Not necessarily, except in a general sense. They both bring great pain and suffering to another human being, the suffering continues long after the actual experience, and they are punishable under the law."

I hear the anger in Paula's voice and stop my writing to look up at her. I wonder if she has been raped or abused. I touch the sore spot on my cheek, fingering it gently so as not to rub off any of the cover-up make-up.

About five minutes before the bell is to ring, Ms. Woods gives us our assignment.

"Copy three of these questions from the board and write a paragraph about each of them. Don't worry about right or wrong answers. Write your opinions, and the reasons you think the way you do. Paula will be back tomorrow and we'll continue this discussion."

I turn to a fresh sheet of paper and write:

1. Is rape a sexual act, or an act of violence?
2. Is rape more likely to occur with a stranger or with some- one the victim knows?
3. Is there such a thing as rape in marriage?

I walk to my next class alone. Even though I'm a senior, I'm pretty new to Hamilton High. I've moved around a lot. My mom works for the racetracks, not with the horses or anything like that, but selling tickets to bettors and cashing tickets for the winners. She sells a lot more than she cashes in. A few years ago she had a chance to stay in one place, at Santa Anita, and not be moving around all the time. It made me really mad that she didn't even consider me when she made her decision.

"I *hate* moving all the time," I told her.

She just shrugged. "I like to keep on the move," she said. Then she told me she'd see me later, she was going out with "the girls."

Anyway, most of my life I've not been in any one school for over three months. It's hard to keep friends that way, so I'm kind of a loner. Mostly, I guess, my friends have been books. Like that book *Are You There, God? It's Me, Margaret.* I learned a lot from that book. And *Of Mice and Men.* I don't know why I like that book so much. It always makes me cry, the ending is so sad. But it seems like an old friend to me, too.

My best real-person friend since third grade was a guy, Sean Ybarra. His mom works for the tracks, too, so we always ended up at the same schools. He was a really good friend — someone I could talk to about anything. But Rudy freaks out if I even glance at another guy, much less talk to them. So I've kind of lost touch with Sean. The last time I talked to my mom, about ten months ago, she said Sean was signed up to join the Conservation Corps. I'll probably never see him again.

Hamilton Heights is the longest I've lived in any one place. After Cheyenne was born, Rudy's mom said the baby and I could move in with them. My mom thought it would be a good idea, so Cheyenne would know her father and all, and besides, she told me, it was hard enough for her to support herself and me, much less adding a baby to all of her financial responsibilities. She wasn't mean or anything, but I sort of got the idea she didn't want me and Cheyenne tagging along with her if there was someplace else we could go.

So, I've been living with Rudy and his mom, Irma, since Cheyenne was four months old. I don't think Irma was dying to have us move in with her, either. Rudy wanted us though, and with Irma it's pretty much what Rudy wants, Rudy gets. He's her youngest son. The two older boys live in Texas now, so Rudy's it. But Irma's okay. She's crazy about Cheyenne, so that's something.

Anyway, I've been at Hamilton High long enough to have friends. It's just that I'm so used to being a loner I don't know how to be anything else.

After school I get in the yellow Teen Moms van and ride to the Infant Care Center with Christy and Janine. I guess they are the closest to being my friends of anyone at school. We always talk about our babies. Janine's baby, Brittany, is two months older than Cheyenne, so I usually know what's coming next. Brittany started walking, and then two months later, Cheyenne started walking. Brittany started saying "no" to everything, and about two months later, Cheyenne started saying "no" to everything. They seem to be following a pattern. Except Cheyenne already says more words. Secretly, I think she's smarter than Brittany, but Janine thinks Brittany's some kind of genius. I guess that's how moms are. Some moms anyway. Maybe not my mom.

We get out of the van at the center and walk inside. This is my favorite time of the day, when I watch Cheyenne, her blond curly hair falling over her face, playing on the floor, or sitting at the table with juice and graham crackers. She's got hair like mine, only mine's darker now than it was at her age. And she has blue eyes, the same as me. But she's built like Rudy, short and stocky.

I watch, loving her, and then the moment comes when she first sees me and her face brightens with her biggest smile. She runs to meet me and I kneel down so she can reach her arms around my neck.

"Mommy, Mommy," she says, and I hug her and twirl her around. Brittany and Ethan come running to their moms, too.

"Cheyenne's had a runny nose today," Bergie (Ms. Bergstrom)

says. "Be sure to check her temperature before you bring her out tomorrow."

"Okay," I say.

"Brittany, too," Bergie says, turning to Janine.

I give Bergie my homework packet. A requirement for having Cheyenne in the Infant Care Center while I go to school is that I have to be involved in a parenting class. The unit I'm working on now is discipline for toddlers. It helps me understand things better. Like how even little kids need to have some say over their own lives. I wish Rudy were taking the parenting class with me, because we disagree a lot. He thinks I spoil Cheyenne, and I think he says no just to be saying no. He plays with her though, and makes her laugh. I think my mom was right about Cheyenne needing to be around her dad, even if Mom was mainly saying that to get rid of us.

Cheyenne gets her backpack, with diapers, a change of clothes and empty bottles, and walks with me to the van. The other two moms carry their kids' backpacks, but Cheyenne always wants to carry her own. At the van, Cheyenne clutches her backpack with one hand and tries to get a grip on the first step with the other hand.

"Can I help you?" I say, reaching down to lift her into the van.

"No! Baby help!" she says, frowning at me. She manages to get one knee onto the lower step, reach the railing with her free hand and pull herself up to the next step, still juggling the backpack. She walks determinedly down the aisle and climbs into her favorite seat, the next one up from the back.

"Baby help" was one of the first things Cheyenne learned to say. One day when she was only about a year old, I started to help her into her car seat. She started crying in frustration, saying, "Baby help, baby help." At first I didn't understand what was wrong, or what she meant. Finally, I got it. I lifted her out of her seat, stood her on the driveway beside the car, and let her climb back in on her own. It's been "Baby help, baby help," ever since.

"I believe that is the most determined child I've ever seen," Bergie says with a smile. I know that's saying a lot, because Bergie's been in charge of the Infant Center for a long time, and she's known hundreds and hundreds of kids.

"I'm proud of her," I say. "You should see her fixing her cereal in the morning if you think getting in the van is determined."

"Well, good for her," Bergie says. "We all need to be determined in this world or we're lost."

I walk down the aisle and take my place beside Cheyenne. She already has her safety belt buckled.

"Mommy. Buckle," she says.

"Okay, okay," I say, kissing her on top of her head.

"Buckle!"

I buckle my belt, wondering at how insistent she is that I buckle-up. I don't think either Ethan or Brittany notice any of that stuff.

Once out on the road, Cheyenne starts sucking her wrist, a sign that she's sleepy. Riding in a car always makes her sleepy. I get my folder out of my backpack and check tonight's assignments. Suddenly there is the blast of an air horn and blinking lights behind us. Cheyenne jumps wide awake, startled. The van driver pulls over to the side of the road and a huge fire truck goes whizzing by.

"WOW!" Cheyenne says, watching with bright eyes.

"WOW!" Ethan and Brittany say.

We all laugh. Now I understand what Bergie means when she says these are the "wow" kids.

2

Rudy's car isn't in the driveway when Cheyenne and I get out of the van. I'm glad. Maybe his boss finally gave him more hours. Rudy gets frustrated because we never have enough money. Like right now he wants new speakers for his car stereo but he can't afford the kind he wants. I get a welfare check once a month, but, except for a few dollars for clothes for the baby, that all goes to Irma to help with food and household expenses.

There's a note on the refrigerator from Irma, telling me to do the dishes from last night and to put away the clothes in the dryer — her dishes and her clothes. She works part-time at Kinko's and she's always too tired to do anything else. I do all the housework and laundry. I don't care, but it seems like she could at least say please or thank you now and then. On the other hand, I guess it was nice of her just to take us in. I know she feels crowded sometimes. We all do. The house is two bedrooms, one bath, a tiny kitchen and a small living room. The four of us, and our stuff, definitely fill up every inch of space.

No matter how annoyed I get with Irma at times, I have to

admit she's a really good gramma. She's never too tired to play with Cheyenne.

"Juice, Mommy," Cheyenne says.

I pull her high chair up close to the counter, where I can watch her, and give her a cup of apple juice. I fill the sink with hot sudsy water and wash Rudy's and Jerry's beer mugs, from last night. I blow dishwater bubbles for Cheyenne and finish Irma's dinner dishes. Then I take the baby from her high chair, change her diaper, and wash her hands and face. After that, I gather up her toys and my books and take her into the living room where she can play while I do my homework.

When Cheyenne's in a good mood, like today, I can do homework and watch her at the same time. But when she's fussy, no way can I concentrate on anything but her. I don't feel sorry for myself or anything. I love Cheyenne with all my heart. It's just hard sometimes, being a mom so soon.

Sometimes when I look out the window of the van on my way to get Cheyenne after school, I see other kids playing sports, or practicing drill team routines, and I wonder how my life would be if I weren't already a mother. The others seem so free, and for me, there's never any let up of responsibility.

It's nearly six o'clock when I hear the rattle of Rudy's loose and leaky muffler. I carry Cheyenne to the window. She laughs when she sees the battered gray Ford.

"Daddy's car!"

We walk to the door to meet Rudy.

"Hi, beautiful women," he says, giving us each a peck on the cheek. I don't smell beer.

"Hey, Missy. Old Murphy wants me to work full-time on this new remodel job he just got. In two weeks, I should have some bad sounds in my car," he says, smiling, giving me the thumbs up sign.

"How about it, Baby," he says, taking Cheyenne from my arms and holding her high over his head. "You and Daddy'll go cruisin' and blast out the oldies, huh?"

Cheyenne smiles and a big glob of drool lands on Rudy's forehead.

"Thanks, Cheyenne," Rudy says sarcastically, handing her back to me. But he smiles. I think we're going to have a good evening.

"Maybe you should get your muffler fixed before you put money into new speakers," I say.

"Nah. That muffler will last for a while. I want something *I* want for a change."

"What about school, if you start working full-time?" I ask.

"Ah, shit, Melissa. It's just that Independent Studies crap anyway. It doesn't mean anything."

"But it's a way to get a diploma," I say.

"I can learn more from Murphy. You and your diploma, anyway. You gonna be ashamed of me if I don't get that piece of paper?"

"No. It's just that, well, later on you might need it."

"Then I'll worry about that later on," he says. "What's for dinner?"

"I don't know. I haven't started it yet."

He gives me that look, like a cloud just settled on his face and a storm may be coming up. "How come you never have dinner ready for me when I get home?"

"I never know what time you'll be here."

"You could at least have stuff started."

"Yeah, well if I'd started anything last night it would have been burned to a crisp by the time you got home."

We could fight. I can feel it. I don't want to, but it might happen. We look each other in the eye, then I look away. Rudy reaches out and touches my cheek, on the spot with the cover-up make-up.

"Come on, Missy, let's go to Domenico's and get a big old pepperoni and cheese pizza."

"Pizza?" Cheyenne says.

We both laugh. The cloud has lifted.

I grab sweatshirts for me and the baby and we walk together to the car. Rudy starts to lift Cheyenne into the car seat.

"Baby help! Baby help!" she says, pushing at him.

"Okay, okay," he says and puts her down.

We stand and wait while she struggles to climb into the car, then into the car seat.

"At this rate Domenico's will be closed by the time we get there," Rudy says, jiggling his keys. He's not as impressed with Cheyenne's determination as I am.

At the restaurant we take a corner booth at the side, away from everyone else. Cheyenne likes to hang over the back of the booth and check out whoever is there and whatever they're eating. Sometimes she likes to sing the ABC song for them. Some people think it's cute and some don't. The corner booth is safest for us.

Late that night, after Cheyenne is sound asleep in her crib and Rudy and I are stretched out in bed, he turns to me and puts his arms around me.

"Now that I'll be making more money, let's go to Vegas and get married," he whispers. "How about next month?"

Getting married is something we've talked about doing since before the baby was born, but for some reason we never get around to it.

"Things will be better when we're married because then I'll know you're mine for sure," Rudy says.

"Okay," I say, thinking of how Melissa Anne Whitman looked written out next to my Peer Counseling notes, how pretty the *W* was. "I'll be eighteen next month," I remind him.

"Let's do it on your birthday. That'd be a great birthday present wouldn't it? And then I'd only have to worry about remembering one special day instead of two," he laughs.

"The 27th," I say.

"The 27th it is. I love you, Missy. I don't ever want to hurt you."

I feel tears welling in my eyes. I know he doesn't want to hurt me, it's just that he gets carried away sometimes, especially if he's been drinking.

Rudy is the first person in the world ever to really care about me. Even after three years he still gets worried if I'm not home right on time. And if he has to work on a Saturday, when I'm home from school, he calls me during his lunch time and break times, too, just to see what I'm doing.

I don't always like having to stay home all day just to answer his calls, but then I think how when I lived with my mom I could be gone for days before she'd even notice. Finally, with Rudy and Cheyenne, I'm important to somebody. I hold him close, feeling his heart beat against mine.

"Let's pretend to make another baby," he whispers.

"I'm on the pill, remember?" I whisper back.

"It's just pretend," he says, kissing me long and gentle, being the Rudy I love with all my heart, the Rudy I wish would never change. I slip my nightgown over my head as Rudy strips off his T-shirt and boxers.

"I love your skin against mine," I whisper.

Rudy groans softly, moving his hands to the places only he has ever touched. Quietly, quickly, intensely, we make love. After, when we're lying relaxed in each other's arms I ask Rudy if he thinks there's such a thing as rape in marriage.

"God, you ask the strangest things," he says, groggy. "Where'd you come up with that idea, anyway?"

"We have this guest speaker in Peer Counseling this week. It's one of the questions I copied from the board for homework."

"No way," he says, in his sleepy voice. "One of the reasons a guy gets married is so he can have sex whenever he wants. How could that be rape?"

"But what if the wife doesn't want to?"

"It's part of the bargain," he says. "When you get married you belong to each other."

"I think it can be rape even if the people are married," I say.

"That's your trouble. You think too much," he says. Then I hear his deep, steady breathing and know that he's asleep.

I walk into the Peer Counseling room and take a seat next to Leticia. Even though I am kind of a loner, Leticia and I talk sometimes. She's super friendly, and talkative, so I don't feel so shy with her. Sometimes we eat lunch together. She even invited me to a party at her house once, but Rudy didn't want to go and he doesn't like me to go anywhere without him.

"Which questions did you write about?" she asks.

I open my notebook and read them to her.

"Yeah, I chose that one about are you more likely to be raped by a stranger or an acquaintance. I thought stranger, but my mom thought acquaintance. I guess we'll find out today . . . What did you say for the one about being raped if you're married?"

"At first I thought no, because that's what my boyfriend thinks. But when I talked with the girls from Teen Moms this morning, they said yes, even if people are married it's still rape if a husband forces his wife to have sex against her will."

"So what did you put?"

"I put both answers, because I couldn't decide," I say.

Leticia laughs. "This is the only class on campus where you can get away with that. I doubt that old Horton takes two answers for a math problem — Ah, the answer is x = 1,272. Or else it's x = 8,523. Wouldn't he flip his cookies?"

It is a pretty funny idea. But in this class the actual answers aren't as important as showing that we've thought about the questions. I wish more of my classes were like Peer Counseling.

Ms. Woods checks attendance while Paula gets started discussing yesterday's questions. It is much more likely that a person will be raped, or murdered for that matter, by someone they know than by someone they don't know. And, she tells us, any time a person is forced to have sex against their will, it is rape. Married or not. "And rape has very little to do with sex and a whole lot to do with violence," she says.

"Where I work at the Rape Hotline," Paula continues, "we've found that rape and other kinds of abuse often go together. Many rapists have been abused as children and also, for some reason, many children who have been abused are also raped some time in their lives . . . So, how do you define abuse?"

As in the discussion yesterday, everyone yells out answers while Paula races to write them on the board. Being hit, kicked, shoved, ridiculed, put down, made fun of, are some of the things students come up with.

"My dad is always putting me down — saying I'm lazy, I'll never amount to anything — stuff like that. Does that mean I'm an abused child?" Tony asks. "Can I sue my dad?"

"You can try," Paula says, "but you'd probably need plenty of money for lawyers if you take that approach."

Most of the students laugh, including Tony, but Paula goes on, all serious.

"I don't know how extreme your case is," she says to Tony. "But I do know that the chances are great that a few of you, maybe several, are right now living under abusive conditions — conditions that not only cause you great difficulty now, but will cause you difficulty for years to come. And some of that abuse is physical, and some is emotional, and it's all painful and damaging. And if you're in a situation where someone is telling you day after day that you are no good, that you are worthless, you are in an abusive situation and you need help with it."

The room is absolutely quiet now, as if no one is even breathing. I wonder if it's true that several of us are being abused. I wonder how many secrets are in this room?

"I think maybe the little boy who lives next door to me is being abused," Leticia says. "His mom yells at him all the time. He's really skinny, and he won't even talk to me, like he's afraid of me."

"I'm afraid of you, too," Josh says, and again there is laughter, and the mood lifts.

Paula passes out sheets with the names and numbers of hotlines to call if you suspect someone is being abused, or if you need help yourself. She talks about our responsibility to protect children who have no way of protecting themselves.

"I'm gonna call this hotline as soon as I get home," Leticia says. "Anonymous reporting. Right?"

"Some are anonymous and some you have to leave your name with."

"I'll start out anonymous," Leticia says.

We get a flier from a safe house for battered women. Besides their phone number there are two lists. "NO ONE DESERVES ABUSE" is the first one. It includes physical abuse, put downs, verbal abuse, having possessions damaged, interference with comings and goings, being harassed and spied on, being stalked, and being isolated.

The second list is titled "YOU HAVE THE RIGHT TO" and it lists: Be treated with respect; be heard; say no; come and go as you please; have a support system; have friends and be social; have privacy and space of your own; maintain a separate identity.

I tuck the flier in my notebook and wonder about all I've heard today. I mean, I know hitting and kicking is abuse. Rudy doesn't do that very often, though. And the thing about having privacy and a space of my own, how does anyone have privacy with four people sharing a small two bedroom house? The right to have friends and be social? I think about Sean, and the friendship I've lost.

On Wednesday Cheyenne has a fever so I stay home from school with her. Sometimes Irma helps out at times like these, but she had to be at work early this morning. It is impossible to do any schoolwork or housework with Cheyenne so fussy. I hold her and rock her and watch a talk show. It's about this famous hockey player who beat his wife to death. Well, he hasn't been convicted yet, but it's only obvious. They're comparing it to the O. J. Simpson case, where there was this history of abuse which kept getting a little worse and a little worse, until the wife ended up dead.

This psychologist is saying that for men who hit their wives, or their lovers, murder is a short step away. I turn off the TV and pour a small bottle of juice for Cheyenne. The doctor said the more liquids the better. She sucks at the bottle, listlessly, her usually dancing eyes glazed with fever. God, it scares me when she's sick. I don't ever want her to be hurting, or in danger. I hold her warm body close and rock her gently. I sing her favorite song to her, "The Circle of Life," from "The Lion King." She has a tape of that music and she plays it so often I've memorized the words.

She falls asleep in my arms, but I continue holding her and rocking her, watching her. In three more weeks Rudy and I are supposed to be going to Las Vegas to get married, but I'm not sure. I keep thinking about that abuse stuff. I've never thought about "abuse" or being "battered." I've just thought, Rudy got mad and lost his temper. But abuse, battered, those words sound so extreme. Of course, when he hits me it feels extreme.

3

The first time Rudy ever hit me was just a few months after we'd started being together. He's three years older than I am, so he was eighteen and I was fifteen. I think that time, when we first loved each other, was maybe the happiest time in my life. I was totally inexperienced with boys — not very pretty — and with my Kmart wardrobe, I didn't expect to ever have a boyfriend. But Rudy saw me one day, standing in the rain, waiting for a bus. He offered me a ride. I never take rides with strangers, but I was so cold and wet, and he was so cute, I got in his car, and that was the beginning of it all.

But back to the first day he hit me, I was at the corner, waiting for the bus again, when Sean came running up to me. I hadn't seen him since Santa Anita closed its season the previous spring.

"Hey, Melissa," he said, "you look great. How've you been?"

"Good," I said with a smile, thinking of Rudy. "Really good. How about you?"

"Oh, you know, same old stuff. Listen, I've got to go for a job interview, but I really want to talk to you and get caught up.

Here's my new phone number. Give me a call tonight, can you?"

"Sure," I said. "I want you to hear all about my boyfriend, and I want to know everything you've been doing since I saw you last." It felt so good to be talking to Sean again. I hadn't seen him since his mom got a steady job at the Los Angeles Convention Center and quit working the horse race circuit.

We were just saying good-bye when Rudy came driving past. He made a big U-turn in the middle of the street and stopped in front of where we were talking. He reached over and pushed open the door and told me to get in.

"This is Sean," I said, starting to introduce them, but Rudy pulled me into the car and peeled away before I could even finish my sentence.

"What's wrong?" I said, thinking maybe there was some emergency or something, he was in such a hurry.

"What do you think is wrong?" he sneered.

"I don't know," I said.

"Don't act all innocent with me!"

He pulled the car to the curb, slamming on the brakes.

"What's wrong?" I yelled. "I don't know what's wrong."

He swung his right hand from the steering wheel to my face in an instant. He hit hard, with the back of his hand. I was stunned.

"Don't you ever let me see you talking to no guy on no street corner like you're nothing but a slut."

"That was Sean, my friend from a long time ago," I said, crying, holding my hand over my smarting cheek.

"Yeah, well I'm your friend now. Not Sean, nobody else but me."

I was so hurt, my cheek, yes, but more, deep inside me. For the first time in my life I had felt loved and secure with Rudy, and in one quick blow he'd shattered those feelings.

"I'm taking you home," he'd said that day. "I've got to go to work, but you just stay at your house until I get there later tonight. You got it?"

I nodded.

"What did he give you?" he said.

"Nothing. We were just talking!"

"He gave you something. I saw him hand you something!"

"He just gave me his phone number," I said, taking the piece of paper from my pocket and waving it in front of him. He grabbed it from my hand, tore it into pieces, and threw it out the window.

"You wanna talk to someone on the phone, call me," he said. "Only me."

Once home, I washed my face and put ice on my cheek. When my mom came in from work and asked me what happened, I told her I'd tripped and fallen against a light pole. She just shrugged.

When Rudy came over that evening he asked if I would please go get a bite to eat with him. I had thought we were through, but when I saw the pleading look on his face I followed him to the car. We picked up a couple of burritos and drove back to his house.

"Come on in," he said. "My mom won't be around for a while."

He took a package from the glove compartment and we went inside.

"Sit by me," he said, patting the spot next to him on the couch. I hesitated.

"Come on, please, Melissa. Please, Missy."

I sat down and he pulled me to him. "God, Missy, you're the best thing that's ever happened to me. If you left me, my life wouldn't be worth shit."

He kissed my forehead, then nestled his head against my neck and shoulder. I could feel the warm dampness of his tears against my neck. I reached up and dried his cheeks with my hand.

"I'm sorry. I'm so sorry," he said. "It's just that I love you so much. I'm so afraid of losing you."

He handed me the box he'd taken from his glove compartment. In it was a gold bracelet with a single charm — a heart.

"This is to tell you I promise you, with all my heart, that I will never ever hit you again. I don't want to hurt you," he said.

I took the bracelet and he fastened the clasp for me. I had hope again that someone loved me, that I belonged to someone.

In the past three years Rudy has hit me more times than I can count. I still wear the bracelet, but it doesn't mean much to me anymore. Usually he only hits me if he's been drinking, but lately he's been drinking more than ever. I think if he'd just stop drinking we'd be fine together.

Rudy's mom says I've just got to learn when to keep my mouth shut, like it's my fault when he hits me. I used to think that was right, but I'm beginning to think otherwise.

"He's like his father was," she told me once. "I finally learned how to handle him. I just shut up and stayed out of his way when he was drinking. That's all you have to do."

"Did you end up with a happy marriage?" I asked.

"I wouldn't say we were the picture of happiness, but at least he hardly ever beat the crap out of me after I learned to zip my lip. I guess we were happy enough, though. I missed him after he died."

I don't know. Rudy says things will be better when we're married. He won't need to hit me anymore because he'll know I'm all his. But what if things aren't better when we get married. Then what? Sometimes, though, Rudy is really sweet to me. And I know he needs me. Not many people need me.

Cheyenne's bottle drops to the floor. I take her into our room and put her down in the crib. She stirs a bit, and opens her eyes.

"Look at the birdies, Chey-Chey," I say, twirling the birds on the mobile that's attached to her crib.

She loves to watch the birds. I think it relaxes her too, and helps her fall asleep.

I tiptoe out of the room. Maybe now I can get some reading done. I'm behind in English and history. Sometimes I have a hard time keeping up. Not that I'm stupid, but there's a lot to do, taking care of a baby and doing the housework and laundry for four people. Plus, I've got a lot on my mind.

When Cheyenne wakes in the morning she is bright-eyed again. She stands in her crib, smiles, and says "Up?" just like always. I am relieved to see her feeling better.

Rudy goes to lift her from the crib, but she starts saying, "Baby help! Baby help!" frowning and holding on to the crib slats. I go over and lower the side rail.

"Let her climb out by herself," I tell Rudy.

"Jesus Christ," he says, putting her down. "What's with this kid, anyway?"

"Nothing. She just wants to do it herself," I say.

"Well everything takes twice as long with this baby help crap."

"But she's learning how to do things," I say.

"So?"

"So, do you want coffee before you leave?" I ask, changing the subject.

On Friday, the last day that Paula is going to be in Peer Counseling, she brings the director of a battered women's shelter with her. This woman, Pam, tells us about the way they do things — how they protect women and their children from abusive husbands, how they help them find jobs and housing to get back on their feet. "It's a six week program," she says.

I raise my hand and ask, "What happens after six weeks?"

Leticia looks at me funny, I guess because I never ask questions in class.

"After six weeks they get settled in another place — their own apartment, or some kind of halfway place, sort of a group center."

"How much does it cost?" I ask.

"No one is turned away because of money."

Pam says how hard it is for abused women to break away, and that some end up going back to their husbands or boyfriends.

"Man, I'd never do that," Leticia says. "A guy hits me once, that'd be it. Ancient history."

"Sometimes, in spite of reality, it's hard for women to give up on whatever dream they had of the man who's beating them. These guys can be very charming."

I look at my bracelet, the heart gleaming with sunlight from the window behind me. Charming is right.

A week before we're scheduled to go to Las Vegas, Rudy comes home late. I smell beer on his breath when he kisses me, but he seems to be in a good mood.

"C'mon, come listen to this."

I check on Cheyenne. She's sound asleep, her arm thrown over "Mary," her doll baby. I walk out to the car and sit in it. Rudy turns on the tape player. It's a rap tape that he knows I don't like, with the words over and over saying, "You're my bitch, my bitch, my bitch." He's got it cranked up so loud it hurts my ears. I get out of the car and walk back into the house.

"Hey, what's with you?" he yells.

"I hate that tape, and besides, I think you should have bought a muffler. We're driving all the way to Las Vegas next week and your car sounds like it will barely make it around the corner."

Irma comes in and flashes me her shut-up look but I don't care.

"Oh, you don't like my bitch tape, Bitch?" Rudy says, walking over to where I'm standing.

"No, I don't," I say, not backing away.

"Rudy, Honey, why don't you come in the kitchen and I'll fix you a cup of coffee," Irma says. Rudy pays no attention.

"And you don't like how I spend my money, bitch? The money I work my butt off for?"

"I didn't say that," I tell him. "I'm just worried about the car. I think it might not make it to Las Vegas."

"I told you. You think too much!" he yells.

"You can't tell me not to think, Rudy Whitman!"

"I'll tell you what to do, bitch!" he says. "And you better do it!"

Then he does what I know he's going to do. He hits me. Hard. In the face. I fall backward against the couch. He hits me again, harder. I cover my face with my arms, sobbing.

"Rudy, stop," Irma is saying. "Stop now." She grabs his arm. He shakes her off and raises his fist again, then lowers it. He is red in the face, breathing hard. He spits at me, then goes to our bedroom, turns on the light, and starts rummaging through the drawer where he keeps the money he's been saving for our Las Vegas trip.

"Daddy?" Cheyenne says, waking.

I go into the bedroom, half-covering my face. I don't know how I look, but I'm sure it's nothing I want Cheyenne to see. "Up?" Cheyenne says.

Rudy walks over and picks her up.

"Baby help," she says, pounding her little fists against him. "Baby help," she says, starting to cry.

"Stop with that goddamned baby help crap!" he yells at her. He lifts her from the crib with a jerk. She's screaming now. With a quick, rough movement, he shoves her back into her crib.

"Shut up!" he yells, raising his hand as if to hit her.

I rush to Cheyenne, and swoop her into my arms. Irma runs into the room.

Rudy takes three quick steps toward me, stopping only inches away.

"I've had all I can take of this place — *I* think this and *I* think that. Who gives a fuck what *you* think! And this constant baby help crap! She's as bad as you are!" he says, shoving Cheyenne, jarring her in my arms.

"Rudy! Stop!" Irma yells. "Not the baby!"

I spin away, leaving my back to Rudy, enveloping Cheyenne in my arms. He gives me another shove and walks away.

"I'm outta this nut house," he says.

I turn in time to see him take the money from the drawer and walk out the door.

I hold Cheyenne close, rocking her back and forth. "It's okay, it's okay," I tell her over and over again, but she cries harder and harder.

Irma comes to Cheyenne, smooths her hair, wipes her face.

"Ohhh, Gramma's sweet baby. Daddy didn't mean to scare you. Shhh. Shhh," she croons softly.

When she turns to me, her voice is not soft and crooning.

"I'm telling you, Melissa, you'd better learn when to keep that mouth shut. You know better than to cross him when he's been drinking . . . Are you okay?"

"I don't know," I say, gingerly touching my throbbing cheek.

"Cheyenne's okay," Irma says, turning her attention back to the baby.

"I don't think he hurt her physically if that's what you mean by okay," I say.

I walk into the bathroom and start the water in the tub. I check my face in the mirror. It's already starting to swell. I take off Cheyenne's clothes and my own and we get into the soothing warm water. I check out her legs and butt, stand her up, turn her around, have her lift first one leg, then the other, checking her over.

"It's okay, Baby, you're okay," I tell her. Slowly, as I wash her all over with the soft washcloth and soap, her sobs subside. But even after she stops crying, her little face looks tight and worried. I wash my own face now, very gently. Irma comes in with an ice pack.

"This will help the swelling," she says, then leaves.

After our bath I take Cheyenne back to her crib. I give her a bottle, to soothe her, and I crawl into bed, too. I don't think Rudy will be back tonight. Usually when he leaves like that he stays away for a day or so.

I'm awake most of the night, tossing, turning, thinking. The left side of my face throbs. I refill the ice bag and take some aspirin and try to sleep.

In the morning, I am awakened by Cheyenne's voice calling, "Up?"

I go to the crib and lower the rail so she can climb out. She holds her arms out to me.

"Baby help?" I say to her.

She leans closer to me, frowning. "No baby help. No," she whispers.

I reach for Cheyenne and pick her up, then set her gently on the floor by the crib. I watch her as she stands quietly, as if she is unsure what to do next. I lift her back into the crib.

"Up?" she says, holding her arms out to me.

"Baby help?" I say, wanting so much to see her determined struggle to climb out of the crib by herself.

"No baby help. No," she says, reaching for me.

Again I lift her from the crib. In my head I hear Rudy's furious scream of "Stop with that goddamned baby help crap!" and suddenly the white hot anger I've not felt for myself starts in my belly and moves through my body, filling me from head to toe with a fiery rage, clearing my brain, showing me the way.

I'm getting out of here. I'm getting Cheyenne out of here.

Maybe he could break my spirit. Maybe I didn't have much spirit to begin with. But he won't break Cheyenne. I shove as many clothes into her and my backpacks as I can. Her favorite blanket and her favorite book go into her pack, too. I change and feed her. Irma comes into the kitchen and asks how I am.

"Good," I say. "Really good."

She looks at me as if I'm crazy, but the truth is, for the first time in three years, I'm sane.

"You just be careful what you say when he gets home, and everything will be okay."

"I'll say what I want," I tell her. "I'll think what I want. And so will Cheyenne."

"You're asking for trouble," Irma says.

"I'm asking for a life," I say.

I wipe Cheyenne's face and take the tray off so she can climb from the high chair. She holds her arms out to me.

"Baby help?" I ask.

Still, she holds her arms up, waiting. I take her from the chair, get our backpacks and my notebook, and walk out the door. Halfway to the bus stop, Rudy drives up. He looks at my face.

"I'm sorry. God, I'm sorry," he says. "Get in the car. Let's go talk."

"I've got to get to school, Rudy," I say. "We'll talk tonight. Don't worry."

"You can't go to school with that face," he says. "What'll you tell people?"

"I'll make up a good story," I say. "I've got a lot of them."

"Jesus, Missy," he says, looking as if he will cry. Then he looks at Cheyenne.

"Hi, Baby," he says. She hides her face in my shoulder. "Oh, God," he says.

"Go home, Rudy. Get some sleep. We'll talk this evening."

"Sure?"

"Sure," I say.

I don't feel sorry about making a promise I know I won't keep. I undo the latch on my gold bracelet and let it fall to the gutter.

At the Infant Center I ask to use the phone. I take the number from my Peer Counseling notebook and call. Six weeks. That's not long to try to figure out a new life for me and Cheyenne. But I've got to try.

After I make the phone call, I explain to Bergie what I'm doing, and that someone from the shelter will come to get me and the baby around noon.

"You're doing absolutely the right thing," she says, giving me a long hug. "I've been worried about you. Light poles seemed to be getting in your way more and more often."

"I loved him so much," I say, feeling my throat tighten. "I thought we could make a life. I tried so hard."

Bergie pulls me to her and holds me while I cry, the way I've seen her hold the toddlers.

"He can be so nice. But then he can be so mean."

"Nice doesn't make up for what he's done to your face," she says, handing me a tissue. "You've got to go to a safe place, and Cheyenne needs a safe place, too. Even if he never touches her, if she grows up seeing you pushed around, that's tremendously damaging."

"Will it be bad for her not to be with her father?"

"Not as bad as it would be to grow up around someone who beats on her mother."

I get our file from the top drawer of the metal cabinet and make copies of everything the woman from the shelter has asked for — Cheyenne's medical records, our birth certificates and social security cards. Luckily it's all there so I don't have to go back to Rudy's for it. I put the copies in a folder, stash it in my backpack, and put the original file back where I found it.

Cheyenne, who has been sitting in a high chair eating graham crackers, calls to me, "Mommy. Up?"

4

I sit waiting in a booth at the back of Maxwell's Cafeteria. Cheyenne is in one of those high chairs on wheels, sitting next to me at the end of the table. It is 11:50. In ten more minutes my whole life will change — Cheyenne's, too. My stomach feels fluttery, the way it gets when I know Rudy is getting madder and madder, when I know he's about to hit me. This time, though, my stomach is fluttery because of what I *don't* know. Like, where will Cheyenne and I be sleeping tonight? Will we find nice people where we're going?

"Mama! Yo-yo," Cheyenne says, pointing to a shimmery dish of red jello on a woman's tray.

"Peas!" Cheyenne says, meaning please can she have some jello.

Four dollars and seventy-six cents is all the money I have and I can see from here that a small jello is eighty-five cents. How will I get my next welfare check if I'm not at Irma's to pick up the mail? I wonder if there'll ever be a time in my life when I don't have to worry about money.

I go over and take the tray off, waiting to see what she'll do. She just sits. I lean over to pick her up. She pushes me away.

"No. Baby help," she says softly, climbing down from the chair.

I smile with relief, a smile as big as it can stretch in my hurt face. "Baby help," I say.

"Come on," I say, rolling Cheyenne away from the table.

We go over to the pay phone in the waiting area. I'm sure both Rudy and Irma are at work. If anyone answers I'll just hang up. Luckily, I get the answering machine. It's my own voice.

"You've reached the home of Rudy and Irma Whitman, and Melissa and Cheyenne Fisher. Please leave a message."

"Rudy and Irma," I say, my voice shaking with an awareness that I'm taking a huge step. "Cheyenne and I are going to a safe place, where no one will hit me, or frighten her. I can't take the hitting and yelling and name-calling anymore."

I hang up and wheel Cheyenne over to the cafeteria line.

The woman who is picking me up wanted to be sure we didn't meet at a kids' hang-out, where we'd see anyone who knew me or Rudy. This place is definitely *not* a kids' hangout. It looks to me as if Cheyenne and I are the only ones under seventy in the whole place. There are more canes and walkers here than I've ever seen in one place before, even when it was Senior Citizen Day at the racetrack.

I take a dish of jello and a small carton of milk for Cheyenne, and a banana to share. As I walk past the meatloaf and mashed potatoes, my mouth waters big time.

It's funny how a lot of people have favorite meals that their mom or grandma fixed. Rudy loves the tamales his mom fixes at Christmas-time, and her fried chicken. Better than the Colonel's he always says. But for me, I love meatloaf because it was always my favorite meal at the employee cafeteria at Santa Anita and Del Mar and Bay Meadows. Every racetrack had a good meatloaf.

"This is Bangle Beads," Sean would tease me, pretending we were eating a horse that had run last in a big race. I wish I had enough money for meatloaf, and more than that, I wish I could talk to Sean again.

"What a sweet girl," the cashier says to Cheyenne as I fumble for my money.

"I have a great-granddaughter just about your size," she says. Cheyenne strains to reach the jello.

"Yo-yo!" Cheyenne says, reaching further.

"She's precious," the woman says to me. "How old is she?"

"She turned two last month."

"Na-na," Cheyenne says, pointing at the banana.

The cashier and I both laugh.

"Enjoy these years with her," she says. "They grow up so fast."

It's what old people always say. I *do* enjoy Cheyenne, but life seems so complicated at times, and difficult. I wonder how it would be if this woman were my grandmother, and Cheyenne's great-grandmother. Could we live with her for a while? I never knew either of my grandmothers.

Whenever I asked about them all my mom would say was "Our family's not like one of those TV families. You're better off not knowing them." If I tried to ask more, or to ask about my father, she'd say, "Case closed."

One thing I will never, ever say to Cheyenne is "Case closed." Any question she ever asks me, I'll answer the best I can.

I balance my tray with one hand and guide Cheyenne's high chair with the other. I get a glass of water and two packs of crackers for me. Back at our table, I put the tray out of Cheyenne's reach and offer her a spoonful of jello.

"Baby help!" she demands.

I put two little squares of jello on a small plate and hand Cheyenne a spoon. She grabs a square, mushes it down on the spoon, and eats the whole thing in one bite. She laughs, proud of herself.

The red squares, smooth and clear, are like the translucent red pieces of glass I once saw in a stained glass window. I take a bite and let it melt sweetly in my mouth, then eat a cracker.

"More!" Cheyenne demands.

"What do you say?" I ask.

"More!" she repeats, louder.

"Shhh," I say, noticing the gray heads turning our way from the table across the aisle from us.

"Say please," I remind her.

"More, peas!" she says.

I put two more squares on Cheyenne's plate and put a straw in the milk carton for her. I notice a woman over near the door, scanning the room. She is wearing baggy jeans and a sweatshirt with a teddy bear on the front. Her long, dark hair is held back with a large, silver barrette. She doesn't look like she belongs with the gray haired, polyester pantsuit crowd that eats at Maxwell's. She walks over to our table.

"Melissa?" she says.

"Yes."

"I'm Vicki," she says, extending her hand.

Her handshake is strong and reassuring, like she's someone who knows what she's doing.

"Seen anyone you know?"

I shake my head.

"Feel safe here?"

"Yes," I say, putting more jello on Cheyenne's plate.

"Good. I'd like a bite to eat before we head out."

Vicki checks out the food on the table.

"Aren't you eating?" she asks.

"I'm not hungry," I say, embarrassed to admit I don't have enough money.

"Well, get hungry," Vicki says. "We've got a long ride ahead of us."

Vicki looks long at Cheyenne.

"Hi, Cutie," she says.

To me she says, "It's good you're getting away while she's still a happy girl."

I nod.

Vicki slides a ten dollar bill across the table to me.

"Get me some of that spaghetti with garlic bread, and a green salad. And get yourself something to eat, too. Does the baby need more?"

"I'll get something she likes. We can share."

"Mommy'll be right back," I tell Cheyenne.

Vicki holds the milk carton for Cheyenne, who takes a big swallow and lets some of the milk run down her chin. I pick up a napkin and start wiping up, but Vicki waves me away.

"Get our food. I can handle this," she smiles.

When I return with Vicki's spaghetti and my meatloaf, Cheyenne is almost finished with her jello. I hand Vicki her change, then sit back down. I force myself not to shovel the meatloaf in like some kind of two-legged pig. Not that I'm on the road to starvation or anything. It's just that I was so upset last night, and still this morning, that I forgot to eat.

I put a few small pieces of meat on Cheyenne's plate. She eats those and asks for more. She really likes the meatloaf, too. Maybe someday we can get our own apartment, and she and I can make meatloaf together, and then, when she grows up, she'll have a favorite meal that she remembers me by. Maybe.

"Dessert?" Vicki asks as she eats the last of her spaghetti and bread.

"No, thanks," I say, getting the baby wipes from Cheyenne's backpack and wiping her face, hands, and the high chair tray. We go outside, I lay Cheyenne out on the bench and change her diaper. Vicki takes the wet diaper to the trash, and Cheyenne and I follow her to the parking lot.

"I couldn't take Cheyenne's carseat," I say, as Vicki opens the door to her car.

"Yep," Vicki says. "We always carry carseats. That's a real giveaway, if you're trying to leave home without anyone knowing — oh, yeah, I'm going for a little walk. I'll just carry the carseat with me," Vicki laughs. Then she turns serious. "We all have to leave a lot behind. Some good. Some bad."

Cheyenne sleeps the whole hour and a half it takes to get from Hamilton Heights to the place in the desert.

"It's the safest thing we can do — get people far away from home." Vicki says. "You'll have seventy-two hours in the center, getting settled, arranging the details, then you'll get enrolled at Desert Dunes High School."

I guess I wasn't thinking about how far away I'd be. Or all the people I won't be seeing anymore. I'm sorry I didn't get to say good-bye to Leticia, or to thank Ms. Woods. At least I got to tell Bergie what I was doing.

At Hamilton High, I was finally beginning to feel like I belonged. Then suddenly I have to leave, just like the old days when the Santa Anita meet would be finished and we'd head up north for the next season. Keep moving. Story of my life. Will that be the story of Cheyenne's life, too? I want something different for her, but I'm not sure how to get it. I thought I'd get it with Rudy, but now . . .

Thinking about Rudy gives me an empty, aching feeling. I look out the window, at the dry, sandy landscape, with those funny looking three-pronged cactus things sticking up all over. I'll bet there are snakes out there, and lizards. I don't know if I'm going to like this or not.

"We'll be there in another fifteen minutes or so," Vicki says. "What do you think of our big town, here?"

There is a convenience store with a filling station, a deli, a post office, a drugstore, and a church.

"Desert Dunes," Vicki says. "Palm Springs is only about twenty miles from here. That's where the fancy people go. You ever been there?"

"No . . . How far are we from Las Vegas?"

"I'm not sure. Probably about four hours if we drove the speed limit, which no one does."

"Rudy and I were supposed to go to Las Vegas next week," I say.

Vicki glances over at me, then back at the road.

"To get married," I explain. "We were going to get married."

"You're smart to leave before you get caught in any legal entanglements. It's easier," Vicki says.

I think of Melissa Whitman, how the name looks prettier than Melissa Fisher, and how it's not a bad luck thirteen letter name like the one I was born with. I hope I'm doing the right thing. About this time, back in Hamilton Heights, I'd be getting Cheyenne from the Infant Care Center. We'd go home and play for awhile, just the two of us, before anyone else got there. Maybe I'd do some homework. For sure I'd clean up Irma's dirty dishes and straighten up the house. Then I'd probably start something for dinner.

Tonight would be a good night. We hardly ever have two bad nights in a row. Rudy might bring a little present home for each of us, and we'd take Cheyenne for a walk in her stroller, and talk about our trip to Las Vegas. That's how it would be in my old life with Rudy. But I'm not in that life now.

"This is it!" Vicki says, pulling into the driveway of a yellow stucco house.

The house sits low and flat, with a rock roof and a cement block wall around the backyard. The front yard is sand, with a few cactus kinds of shrubs and a scraggly palm tree. The air is hot and dry — much hotter than I'm used to on a March afternoon. I hear the voices of children from the other side of the block wall.

Vicki picks up the two backpacks while I gently ease my sleeping daughter from the carseat.

"In here," Vicki whispers, pointing to a room off the hallway.

There is a crib, a dresser with a mirror over it, and a single bed. Vicki puts our things on the floor next to the bed.

"Your home for six weeks," she tells me.

It's not really home, though. The closest I ever came to home was Rudy and Irma's, and I left that. Maybe this is all a big mistake.

I hold Cheyenne close for a minute, hoping she will wake up, but she doesn't. I lay her gently into the crib and follow Vicki out of the room and into what might have been a dining room but now is an office with a computer, fax machine, copier, and papers strewn everywhere.

A very large woman, thirtyish, with olive skin and gray-green eyes, takes a stack of papers from a chair and motions me to sit down.

"Carla Martino," she says, extending her hand.

"Melissa Fisher," I respond.

"Vicki will listen for your little one while we take care of business here," Carla says.

Vicki picks up a huge stack of papers and an alphabetical organizer and takes them into the living room.

"Everyone here has work responsibilities," Carla says. "You will, too, after your first three days."

"I don't mind work," I say.

Carla swivels her chair away from the desk and sits facing me.

"Before we get started on this paper work, tell me a little bit about yourself. Why did you decide to come to us?"

I realize I've never even said the words, "Rudy hits me." His mother knew, because she saw it, but we never talked about it except in some hidden way, like when she'd say if I was smart I'd learn to keep my mouth shut. Bergie guessed, because she's the kind of person who notices things, but even when I told her I was coming to the shelter I just talked around things, saying I had to get away, saying I needed a safe place for me and Cheyenne.

"Melissa? Why did you decide to come to us?" Carla repeats.

Her voice is low and gentle, somehow inviting. I take a deep breath.

"Sometimes Rudy hits me," I say.

"And how long has this been going on?"

"Not very much," I tell her.

"No, I mean from the first time he hit you — how long?"

I count back and am shocked by my own answer.

"Almost three years," I say. "But really, it doesn't happen very often."

She looks closely at the bruise on my face. "Once is very often," she says.

"How about the baby? He ever hit her?"

"That's what got me so scared," I say.

I tell Carla about how Rudy grabbed Cheyenne out of her crib last night and then slammed her back into it — how frightened she'd been, and withdrawn for a while. And I'm angry all over again. How could anyone be mean to a helpless baby? Her own father?

"I don't love him anymore," I tell Carla. Then the tears start and I can't stop them.

"He can't love us if he treats us like that," I say, sobbing.

Carla hands me a tissue.

"You're right, Melissa. That's not love."

After I've used up about half a box of tissue, Carla asks, "Do you feel like starting the paper work now?"

"Sure," I say.

"Do you have your birth certificates?"

I go into the bedroom where Cheyenne is still sleeping soundly. I can't believe how long she's sleeping. First in the car and now here. She was pretty restless last night though, after Rudy had scared her so. Maybe she's extra tired today.

I get my backpack, take it back to the office and hand Carla the file with our papers. She makes copies of everything and hands them back to me.

"I don't see a court order for your emancipation here," Carla says.

"Emancipation?"

"Yes. In order for you to stay in the shelter you either have to be an adult, or have a court order that says you're an emancipated minor."

"I'm almost an adult," I say. "I'll be eighteen next week."

"Do you have somewhere else to stay until your birthday?"

"Not really," I say.

What if they don't let me stay? I never even thought of that. In Peer Counseling, and talking with Vicki earlier, no one said anything about emancipation.

"You married? If you're married you're considered emancipated."

"No. We were *going* to get married, but we didn't do it yet."

Carla looks at me intently.

"Legally, we can't give you shelter under these conditions," she says.

"I don't want to go back," I say, imagining the scene if I show up at Rudy's sometime around midnight.

"You shouldn't have to go back," Carla says. "I'm just telling you the bind we're in."

"It's only for a few days, then I'll be an official adult," I say.

"I know. But we've got to do everything by the book. There are people — angry husbands, people in the community who think we're bringing down their property values — who would love to have an excuse to shut us down. Harboring a minor without permission would give them the power to close our doors."

In the background I hear Cheyenne cry out. I rush to pick her up. She is standing in the crib, arms out, her first cry now a full fledged scream.

"Mommy! Mommy!"

I pick her up and hold her close, feeling her heart beat fast against my chest. She seems panicked, maybe from waking up in a strange place. I walk with her through the living room and back to the office.

"It's okay," I tell her, swaying back and forth. "It's okay," though within me it feels as if nothing is okay, or is going to be okay, ever. Carla is on the phone, but she turns and flashes a big, white-toothed smile at me as she sets the receiver back in place.

"Here's the deal," Carla says. "All we have to do is get your parent or guardian to sign a permission form stating that you can stay here and there's no problem. What do you think?"

I am suddenly flooded with relief.

"My mom doesn't care if I stay here," I say. "She was glad when I moved out to stay with Rudy."

"Would she sign a paper saying it's okay for you to be here?"

"For sure," I say.

"Well then, all we have to do is fax this form to her, have her sign it and fax it back."

"Well . . . first we have to find her," I say.

Carla's smile fades and my anxiety comes back.

"She moves around a lot," I explain.

When I talked to her last month she was staying over by the airport, working Hollywood Park. But I'm sure that meet's over.

"Do you have a newspaper — sports section?" I ask.

Carla looks puzzled but digs around under papers and fast-food containers and comes up with the sports page. I bounce Cheyenne on my left hip and thumb awkwardly through the paper. I used to have the sequence memorized — Del Mar is always summertime, I remember that because Sean and I would spend all day at the beach, swimming, sometimes getting into a volleyball game. But then what? September, we started school up north. But where were we in the spring?

"Santa Anita," I say, finding the horse racing section of the *Times*.

"This is a strange time to be thinking of betting a horse,"

Carla says.

I laugh. "No, that's where my mom is working now. If I hurry I can probably get a message to her before she leaves."

"Well, hurry then," Carla says, handing me the phone.

Carla and Vicki entertain Cheyenne with a jack-in-the-box and a toy top that whistles. Soon Cheyenne is squealing with delight.

I leave a message for my mom, saying it is urgent that she call me back as soon as possible. I've never used the word urgent with her before. I guess it works because within a half hour she calls.

"No problem," she says, when I tell her I need permission to stay in a shelter.

"How's the baby?" she asks. She doesn't ask how I am, or why we need to be in a shelter.

"Cheyenne's fine. You wouldn't recognize her, she's grown so much."

There is a pause, then my mom says, "No, I don't suppose I would. What was she the last time I saw her? Eighteen months?"

"Fourteen months. She's two now."

"Well, I'll bet she's changed. Let me give you my phone number, maybe we can get together in a week or two."

I write the phone number down, doubting that anything will come of it.

Carla faxes a form to Santa Anita. My mother signs and faxes it back.

As it comes off the machine, Carla wipes her forehead in a gesture of relief.

"For a while there I was afraid we couldn't let you stay," she says. "It's a good thing your mom was so cooperative."

"My mom's happy for me to stay wherever, as long as it doesn't put her out."

"Well, this time it worked to your advantage."

That's true. Cheyenne and I have a place to stay, officially, for six weeks. Six weeks. Three changes of clothes each. One dollar and eighty-nine cents. That's what I have to show for my almost eighteen years of life. That and Cheyenne.

I sit in a worn vinyl chair, across from Carla's desk, filling out forms attached to a clipboard. I answer question after question about my past life and my present situation. Cheyenne, still fascinated by the top and working to make it spin, sits on the floor beside me.

From somewhere in another part of the house I hear the familiar sounds of "Sesame Street." I pause to listen, knowing by heart what pictures go with the words and songs. *I* want to live somewhere like Sesame Street, where Cheyenne can be safe and happy, and where people love each other, and no one ever hits anyone else. Living with Rudy was a long way from Sesame Street, but Desert Dunes doesn't seem much closer. Right now, I feel all lonely, and empty, and I'm not even sure I should have come here.

I pick Cheyenne up and hold her close.

"Love you," I whisper.

"Yuv you," she says, snuggling down, nestling her sweet face against my neck.

I feel tears starting again, but I take a deep breath and stop them. No matter what's ahead, I'll stay strong for Cheyenne. I put her back down on the floor and pick up the top to give it a spin.

"No! Baby help!" she says, taking the top from my hand and trying to spin it.

I laugh.

"Finished?" Carla says.

I take the forms to her desk. She checks to be sure everything is complete.

"I'll fax your address change to Social Services tomorrow — Did you read this agreement carefully before signing it?" she asks, turning to the last page on the clipboard.

"Yes," I say.

"So you understand that most of your welfare check covers food and housing for you and Cheyenne. There won't be much left over for luxuries."

I laugh. "There never is."

"And do you also understand that we're very serious about zero tolerance for drugs and alcohol here?"

Bam! I feel a sharp jab at my ankle and look down to see Cheyenne raising the top to hit me with it again.

"Cheyenne! No!" I tell her, grabbing the top and prying it from her hands.

"Mine!" she screams.

"Not to hit with!"

I pick her up. She struggles to get down.

"Mine. Mine. Mine," she chants, leaning toward the floor where the top sits.

I turn her face toward me. "Look at me, Cheyenne. No hitting. Remember?"

"Okay," she says, moving toward the top.

"Okay what?"

"No hit."

I let her slide back down on the floor. She lifts the top, as if she might hit me again. Then she smiles at me, puts it back on the floor, and works to make it spin.

"You're good with her," Carla says.

"It's so hard sometimes," I say.

"I know — once you're a mom there's no let up from responsibilities."

We both watch Cheyenne for a moment, then Carla says, "Let's get back to our zero tolerance talk. Drugs, alcohol — one slip and you're out. The same with doing *anything* to reveal where you're staying. These things jeopardize the whole group, and that's where we part company."

"No problem," I say.

"Good," Carla smiles. She rises from her chair and stretches her long, muscular arms toward the ceiling, revealing the slogan on her T-shirt, *"What about 'No' don't you understand?"* She bends, legs straight, and touches her palms to the floor, then straightens.

"Getting the kinks out," she says. "Come on, I'll introduce you around. We're a quirky group here, and we're all working through some heavy stuff, but I think you'll feel at home in no time."

"Home," I think, wondering if I've ever really felt at home anywhere, wondering what the word even means.

5

I'm in the recreation room, sorting through used baby clothes, taking out the size twos that I think will work for Cheyenne. Six of the other "survivors" are also in the room. There's Lori, built like a football player, sprawled out on the couch, half asleep. She sleeps a lot, so I haven't really talked with her much, yet.

Alice, Trish and Sandra are playing cards. Alice and Trish are both black, but the similarity stops there. Alice is big and sort of tough talking. Trish is slim and stylish looking, and soft spoken.

In the corner, away from the card game, Carla is talking seriously with someone whose name I've forgotten. A couple of the older kids are playing quietly on the floor.

Right now, Cheyenne's in the play yard with Kevin and his mother, Daphne. Of the twelve other girls, women I guess I should say, who are living here, I like Daphne best. She's nearest my age, nineteen, and she's serious about being a good mother to Kevin.

Cheyenne and Kevin are already friends, even though they've only known each other for two days. He's almost three, but Cheyenne keeps up with him pretty well.

I find a yellow playsuit, a white T-shirt, sandals, and jeans. That's a good start. Maybe bleach will get the stains out of the T-shirt.

I'd like to sneak back into Irma's house and get the rest of our clothes and Cheyenne's toys, but I have no way to get there. Besides, the shelter has a rule against going anywhere near the abuser's territory. There are a lot of rules here. I can't leave this place, even to walk to the store, for another day. And no phone calls yet, either.

The way Carla explained things to me, the first seventy-two hours are a very important break from my old life. After the seventy-two hour transition period, there's more freedom, but we're not supposed to have any contact at all with "the abuser" for the whole time we're here. It's weird thinking of Rudy as "the abuser," even if he was.

My thoughts are abruptly interrupted when the peaceful buzz in the rec room is shattered by Alice yelling at her daughter.

"Get your butt over here when I call you!"

Kamille sits on the floor in front of the TV, dressing a one-armed Barbie doll, as if she's not even heard her mother's demand.

"If I have to get up out of this chair and come for you I'll kick your fat ass . . . "

"Alice, remember . . . ," Carla starts.

"Oh, Christ!" Alice says, rising heavily from her chair, stomping out of the room, and slamming the back door so hard the kitchen windows rattle.

Carla follows Alice, closing the door softly.

Kamille sits, not turning her head, stuffing tiny pieces of rolled up paper into Barbie's empty sleeve, trying to make it look as if Barbie has both arms.

"C'mere, Honey," Trish says, motioning to Kamille.

Kamille continues to be absorbed in her play, not looking up.

"I think I can help you with your doll," Trish says. "I'm sort of a doll doctor."

Kamille picks up the doll and goes to stand beside Trish.

"Ummm. We'll have to make a prosthesis," she says.

Kamille looks at her questioningly.

"Big word, huh, Kamille," I say, folding the baby clothes we can't use and putting them back in the plastic container.

Kamille watches me, smiling shyly. She has coffee colored skin and big black eyes that, when they meet mine, make me want to shield her somehow from her mother's cutting words.

I go outside to check on Cheyenne, leaving Trish and Kamille at work on a pipe cleaner prosthesis for Barbie.

"**M**ommy! Watch this!" Cheyenne yells when she sees me standing next to Daphne in the play yard.

"Watch 'Yenne," Kevin echoes Cheyenne's demand.

"I'm watching. I'm watching!" I say, laughing.

Cheyenne climbs to the top of the slide, balancing precariously at the top. I hold my breath, fearing a fall. She turns and smiles at me, then climbs onto the slide and whizzes down, screaming in delight.

She lands in the soft sand, rolls, jumps up and says, "See?"

I clap my hands. "What a big girl you are!"

"And brave," Daphne says.

Carla is talking earnestly to Alice at a picnic table on the other side of the yard. I can't hear what Carla is saying, but Alice, crying, keeps saying over and over, "I know, I know."

Daphne and I sit under a tree, watching the kids, telling each other our stories.

"I was sixteen when Kevin was born," Daphne says. "Same as you and Cheyenne. My mom and dad are real religious and they wanted me to marry Dean. That's what he wanted, too. He's twelve years older than I am, and it's like all the grown-ups around me knew what was best. So I just married him. What else could I do?"

Kevin comes running over, crying, "Yenne, Yenne."

"What, Kevin?" Daphne asks.

"Yenne won't let me go down the slide," he whimpers.

I see Cheyenne, standing on the top step of the slide, gripping the sides, blocking the way to anyone else who might want to use it.

"Come on, Kevin," I say.

He takes my hand and I walk him over to the slide.

"Go on down, Chey-Chey, so Kevin can have a turn, too," I tell her.

"No! My slide."

"No, it's not your slide. It's everybody's slide and you have to take turns."

Kevin starts crying again.

"Cheyenne!"

"No!"

"Do you want time out?"

"No!" she screams, louder.

"Let Kevin have his turn then!"

"No!"

I let go of Kevin's hand, pry Cheyenne's hands loose from the slide and carry her into the house. Putting her in the crib in our room, I walk out and shut the door.

"Mommy! Sorry!" she cries, as if her heart is breaking.

I can hardly stand it, but I know I have to leave her in there for at least three minutes to get her mind off of being the boss of the slide. The second hand on my watch drags slowly, thirty seconds, one minute, to the point at the bottom of the bright red heart, then around to the top. Rudy bought the watch for me at the County Fair, back when I was first pregnant. It's a reminder of better times.

Three minutes. I open the door and hold my arms out to Cheyenne.

"Up?"

I lower the crib side and let my "baby help" daughter climb out by herself. Then I squat down beside her.

"Are you ready to take turns on the slide now?"

"Yes," she says, all serious.

I grab a tissue and wipe her tear-stained cheeks and runny nose, then we go out to the play yard to try again. Kevin and Daphne are sitting on one of the little benches. Kevin is carefully picking small pieces off a banana and placing them in Daphne's mouth.

"I feel so strong," she laughs. "Now, your turn."

She breaks a piece off a banana and puts it into Kevin's open mouth.

"Ever since I told him bananas are good for you, he insists on sharing his bananas with me . . . What a sweetie," she says, kissing the back of Kevin's neck.

Later, when both our kids are down for naps and we've finished the kitchen clean-up, Daphne and I get sodas from the machine and go back outside. The sky is bright blue, with billowy clouds floating slowly from north to south. The air is dry and warm.

Back in Hamilton Heights the air is probably heavy with smog and the sky is probably gray. I like seeing a blue sky, but Desert Dunes still seems like a foreign land to me.

"I'll be leaving here in two weeks," Daphne says.

"To where?"

"Probably one of the halfway houses, but I'm scared I'll want to go home. I know that would be stupid, but I miss my mom, and my dog," she laughs a tiny little laugh and looks away.

"Do you miss home?" she asks me.

"I miss something," I tell her. "I'm not even sure what it is, though. It's not like I really have a home."

Daphne gets up and goes into the house. She comes back with pictures.

"Here's all of us," she says.

Her mom is wearing a dress and smiling sweetly. Her dad's in a suit and tie and so is her husband, Dean. Daphne's dressed up, too, holding a much younger Kevin, who's squinting his eyes against the sun.

"This was just after church, the day Kevin was christened."

"Everybody looks so nice," I say.

She nods, then shows me another picture of her dog, Cinnamon, and her cat, Nutmeg. Fanning out the next three pictures, like a hand of cards, she holds them in front of me. At first I don't even recognize her.

"My god."

The pictures are in color, two front shots, one showing more of her left side and the other showing more of her right. The third picture is taken from the back. She's naked. The front shots show her face, swollen and bruised, and an ugly grapefruit sized bruise on her upper arm. Her left breast has a purple bruise the size of a silver dollar, and her upper thighs are bruised and swollen looking.

The back view shows both sides of her butt, bright red, bloody in places, where her husband kicked her repeatedly with his work boots. The pictures make anything Rudy did to me seem like love pats.

"I keep these to remind me of what follows the family church day scene," she whispers. "They took these pictures at the hospital."

"Was that just before you came here?" I ask.

"No. These pictures were from about six months ago."

"You went back to Dean after that?"

She nods her head yes and gives that funny little laugh of hers.

"My father thought I should. He said if I would learn to submit to my husband, like the Bible says, everything would be fine."

Then Daphne shows me the last picture. It is of a high school swim team, with her in the middle, smiling broadly, wearing a first place medal around her neck.

"Before and after," she says, putting the smiling image next to the front shot picture of her horribly bruised self.

"You were a swimmer?"

"A high school champion, until I got pregnant. That changed everything . . . I was so stupid," she says. "Dean was a youth director at a church camp. All the girls had crushes on him, but he chose me. I felt so important. And I thought anything he wanted to do must be all right, because he was almost like a minister. Stupid, stupid, stupid me," she says.

"Me, too," I sigh.

"I wish I could step back into that picture and start over again from there," Daphne tells me.

"I don't even know where I'd want to start over again from," I say. "Sometimes I wish I'd never met Rudy, but I don't want to wish Cheyenne away, and without him, she wouldn't be here."

"Sometimes I wish I'd gone to one of those homes for pregnant girls where they arrange adoptions. I mean, I love Kevin with all my heart, but what chance do I have to give him a good life? And what chance do *I* have?"

We sit quietly for a while, each with our own questions about our lives.

"I'd better check on Cheyenne," I say.

"Listen for Kevin, too, would you?"

Everything is quiet in Kevin's room, but I hear Cheyenne singing the Barney song. "I love you, you love me, we're a happy family . . . "

Most of the time I'm fine. But sometimes, like now, things feel all shaky inside me, like my whole insides are shifting and maybe something's going to break, or get disconnected.

When it's time to start dinner preparations, Daphne and I take our kids to the rec room where Trish has child care duty. I'm glad it's Trish and not Alice. I wouldn't want to leave my dog with Alice, much less my daughter. Not that I have a dog, but that's just how I feel about Alice. She's got a mean streak that I don't want Cheyenne to be around without me to protect her.

I've never lived with so many people before, but I guess I'll get used to it. The house we're in has the main kitchen and office and play yard, with only three bedrooms. Cheyenne and I have a room to ourselves and so do Daphne and Kevin. The other bedroom, the biggest one, has four beds in it. That's where Trish, Lonni, Sandra, and the other one whose name I've forgotten all sleep.

Next door is where the others stay. Everything but the kitchen over there has been converted to bedrooms, so there are beds in the living room and dining room, besides in the regular bedrooms. Six women and three kids stay next door. Everyone eats here, though. Carla seems to be around almost all the time, but she doesn't live here like the rest of us do.

I'm glad Daphne and I have kitchen duty together. She's easy to work with. Not like some of the others.

Preparing food for twelve adults and five children is a big task. We get out the notebook with the recipes in it and find the one for Thursday, which is spaghetti night. Cheyenne will like that, but she's a good eater, anyway. So far, except for peas, she's liked everything I've tried feeding her.

I'm frying a huge batch of hamburger while Daphne's dumping stuff for the sauce into a pan.

"Hand me the oregano," Daphne says.

I find it on the seasoning shelf next to the stove and hand it to her. Back at Irma's we have a small container of oregano, but here all of the seasonings are in extra large sizes.

Carla comes into the kitchen and checks the recipe.

"Use more garlic," she says to Daphne.

"The recipe doesn't even say garlic, just garlic salt," Daphne says.

"Ay, what's an Italian girl to do? Spaghetti without garlic?"

Carla is rummaging through the cupboards, in search of garlic I guess, when there is a stream of cussing coming at us from the office in the next room.

"My ass! If I wanted to know what you thought, *bitch*, I'd have asked! Don't be giving me none of your shit!"

"And don't *you* be spouting off your foul mouthed talk to me . . . "

Carla turns and rushes into the office, where Alice stands in the doorway, hands on hips, facing someone I can't see from where I'm standing.

"Okay. Alice, take a seat. Trish, you, too." Carla says, pointing in the direction of the living room.

"We won't be watching 'Friends' tonight," Daphne says with a sigh. "That's the one program I care about and this is three weeks in a row that Alice has messed things up."

"What do you mean?" I ask, puzzled by what Alice has to do with Daphne watching "Friends."

"Group meeting after dinner tonight. We'll have to deal with *tensions*," she says with a touch of sarcasm.

"We aren't tense," I say. "Why can't *we* watch 'Friends'?"

"When Alice is tense, everyone's tense. The trouble is, Alice is *always* tense. Besides, whenever there's an argument, or someone has a complaint, the whole group deals with it."

"Being a community," I say, quoting the pamphlet Carla gave me to read when I first got here.

"Right. We're a community, but we're not exactly in Mr. Roger's neighborhood."

"And we don't live on Sesame Street, either," I say.

Daphne laughs her short, funny little laugh.

"Let's get the bread into the oven and then we can do the salad," Daphne says.

After dinner and clean-up, we all gather in the living room, chairs in a circle.

"Five deep, cleansing breaths," Carla says.

We all sit straight and breathe in slowly and deeply, then let go in long exhales. It's as if we are all one giant organism, all using the same lungs.

"We have a problem to deal with here," Carla says.

"Only one?" Sandra says.

Most of the others laugh. Carla goes on.

"Remember," she says, "no swearing, no disrespect. Use 'I' statements to say how you feel, none of those accusing 'you' statements. And another reminder. Everything that's said in this group is strictly private and confidential . . . So . . . Do you want to start, Trish?"

"Let Alice start," Trish says, not looking up.

"Okay by me!" Alice says, her black eyes flashing anger. She looks kind of like a fat Whoopi Goldberg, but without a sense of humor.

"First, it pisses . . . "

"No swearing, please," Carla says.

"Okay! It *pickles* me off when a *fudgin'* goody two shoes *witch* like Madame *Patricia* here tries to tell me how to handle my own kid. She's never *had* a kid so what does she know?"

I can feel the intensity of Alice's anger clear across the room, and it's not even directed at me.

"You don't have to *have* a child to understand that calling a child names and telling her she's stupid is a terrible thing to do," Trish says.

"Try that with an 'I' statement," Carla says.

Trish thinks for a moment. Her hair is long and neatly pulled back in a tortoise shell barrette. She undoes the barrette, runs her fingers through her hair, then clamps the barrette back on.

"I . . . " Trish stops, then thinks a bit longer and starts over.

"I feel sorry for Kamille when you . . . when she hears her mother call her names."

"She's used to it," Alice says. "And she may as well stay used to it because that's how life is. Bitch, fat ass, stupid, I grew up on it and it didn't hurt me."

Lonni sighs loudly.

"Lonni?" Carla says.

"I think names *do* hurt. I feel hurt, too, when I see the look in Kamille's eyes when the name calling starts. And I bet the names hurt you, too, Alice, if you could admit it."

Alice turns sideways in her chair, facing away from Lonni.

"Maybe we could go around the room and just tell an experience we've had in which someone's called us a name, and how we felt about it."

As soon as the group session is over I get Cheyenne from the rec room and give her a bath. Then I take her to our room, where we curl up on my bed and read from her favorite book, *Brown Bear, Brown Bear, What Do You See?*

She points and says, "Brown Bear," then "Red Bird," then "Yellow Duck," until we get to the last two pages, where she points and identifies each animal all over again.

"More," she says.

"No. Bedtime."

"Mommy's bed," she says.

"Well, okay, if you'll go to sleep," I tell her.

I turn back the covers and lay her down on the side next to the wall, then get undressed and into the oversized T-shirt I'm using for pajamas. I climb into bed beside Cheyenne. She is on her side, facing me. I smell the clean scent of her baby skin.

"Night, night," I say, kissing her soft cheek.

"Night, Mommy," she says, closing her eyes.

It is not until I hear Cheyenne's steady, sleeping rhythm of breathing, that my mind wanders back to the group meeting — all the awful names people were called when they were children and still so tender. I will never tell Cheyenne that stupid rhyme, the one I used to believe, "Sticks and stones will break my bones but names will never hurt me."

Even Daphne's father, who's supposed to be so religious, called her names. "Satan's Tool," "Anti-Christ," "Crucifier."

Nobody really ever called me names until I got together with Rudy, then he made up for lost time. My mom wasn't a great mom, but at least she never called me names. She never even seemed to get mad at me. I guess it was more like I was invisible to her. Maybe that's worse than being called names. One thing makes you hurt and angry, and the other makes you feel like you're made of air, like people could just walk right through you without noticing. I didn't feel like air with Rudy. He noticed.

Cheyenne stirs slightly and rests her left hand on my cheek. I'm more than air to Cheyenne.

Tomorrow I register at my new high school. I hope I like it as much as I liked Hamilton High, but that's not possible. It takes a long time to like a school that much. I'm back to my old keep moving pattern, but now Cheyenne has to keep moving, too. Thinking about Brittany and Ethan and Bergie, and how comfortable Cheyenne was at the Infant Care Center back in Hamilton Heights, I wonder how she'll respond to a new center.

Sometimes I wish I'd grown up with religious parents, like Daphne did. I don't mean *her* parents, but someone who'd taught me to pray. It seems like that might be better than wishing on a star, but I don't know how it works. I ease my way out of bed and go to the window. I'll say one thing for the desert, there are a lot more stars out here than there are back home — Hamilton Heights, I mean. It's not really home.

I find the brightest star and wish that Cheyenne will like the new Infant Center, and that I'll like my new school. I wish Alice would stop calling Kamille names, and that someday I can work things out so Cheyenne and I can live some place nice where people love us and where there's no hitting, or name calling, or mean, nasty anger.

"Amen," I say, even though I know you're not supposed to say that to a star.

6

Vicki, the person who met me at Maxwell's Cafeteria, shows up at seven-thirty Friday morning to take me and Cheyenne to Desert Dunes High School.

"How's it going?" she asks, after I get Cheyenne buckled into the carseat and then take my place in the front.

"Okay, I guess. I'm not really used to living with so many people."

"Yeah, that takes a little getting used to, all right," Vicki says. "Group living, bland foods, and no men," Vicki laughs. "It's worth it, though. I'd never have managed to get my life together without being in a shelter for a while."

I turn away from watching the strange flat landscape roll by.

"Do you have your life together now?"

"Pretty much. I've got a job that pays the rent, got my own apartment, nobody's beating on me anymore."

"Truck! Wow!" Cheyenne yells from the back.

"Yeah. Wow!" I smile back at her, still feeling the whish of wind from the big truck and trailer that has just passed us.

"Of course, it'd be harder with a kid," Vicky continues. "I was lucky I didn't have any kids."

Cheyenne smiles up at me. Vicki's idea of luck is different from mine.

"The job I've got now is okay — hostess at Coco's over in Palm Desert — but when I finish the computer programming course I'm taking at City College, I should be able to get something a lot better."

"I thought you worked for the shelter," I say.

"Just volunteer stuff a few hours a week. They helped me out so much, it seems like the least I can do . . . You know what I think helped me a lot?" Vicki says.

"What?"

"Those journal writings they give you."

"I hate doing that," I say. "They're too hard. Like yesterday it was to think of what I want to let go of in my life, and to write down what I can do to make it happen, what tools I need, what support system I need . . . I didn't even know where to start. I mean, I guess I want to let go of Rudy, but I'm not even sure about that."

She laughs. "Journals make you think, that's the hard part. It's the important part, though. You've got to get your head screwed on straight, so you'll know not to take any shit from some guy who claims he only hits you 'cause he loves you so much."

"How did you know what Rudy says?"

She laughs again. "They *all* say that. Haven't you heard that in the group meetings?"

"We've only had one group meeting since I've been there, and we talked about how Alice treats her daughter."

"Whoa! Remember the confidentiality rule?"

"Oh, yeah. I guess I just thought . . . "

"Right. I've been through it, but I'm not a part of *your* group. It's okay to talk in general terms, but no names."

"Sorry," I say, embarrassed.

"No big deal," Vicki says, pulling over to the curb and stopping.

"Here we are," she says, pointing to a sign that says "Desert Dunes High School."

There are seven buildings, the kind I think they call "portables," a baseball diamond and a half basketball court. Everything is painted a sandy beige, to match the surroundings I guess.

Vicki walks with me and Cheyenne into the building labeled "Office," and we prepare to wait. That's how it always is at schools. Get there at the appointed time, then wait and wait. I came prepared though, with plenty of toys and juice for Cheyenne, and a book for me. It's this book called *Go Ask Alice* about a girl who's freaking out because she and her parents move and she has no friends. Right now I'm wondering, what's the big deal here? To me, moving a lot and not having friends is sort of business as usual. I can't tell yet if *Go Ask Alice* is going to end up being like a friend to me or not.

After filling out stacks of enrollment forms, and more forms for Cheyenne, we go to the Infant Care Center where Cheyenne will stay while I'm in classes. It's pretty much the same set-up as the Infant Care Center connected with Hamilton High, except I don't know anyone here and neither does Cheyenne.

Vicki arranges to meet me after school is out, and I stay with Cheyenne to help her get used to the new place. Mrs. Seales, the teacher, gives Cheyenne a graham cracker and shows us around. We check out the cribs and the big plastic blocks, the play yard, and sandbox. I laugh when I see the sandbox.

"What's funny?" Mrs. Seales asks.

"The whole play yard is sand," I point out. "Isn't that kind of like a refrigerator in an igloo?"

"I see what you mean," she says, smiling. "But the sand in

the box is clean and fine — a different texture than plain old desert sand."

Cheyenne spots a boy pushing a small red wheelbarrow. She runs over to him.

"My turn!" she yells.

He keeps pushing.

She turns back toward me. "My turn, Mommy!"

Mrs. Seales walks over to Cheyenne, takes her by the hand, and leads her to another look-alike wheelbarrow. Cheyenne pushes it along the walkway, mimicking the boy.

"She'll do fine," Mrs. Seales says.

We watch the kids play while she tells me what's expected of me — how many hours a week I need to help out in the center, when the parenting groups meet and what kind of homework I'll need to do for the parenting class. It really isn't that different from before, except I miss Bergie, and Christy, and Janine.

"When do you start classes?" Mrs. Seales asks.

"Monday. For today I'll stay here with Cheyenne, so she can get used to things."

Mrs. Seales nods. "You'll like Desert Dunes. Have you ever been to a continuation high school before?"

"I've been to about every kind of school there is," I tell her. "I move around a lot."

"Well . . . "

It seems like maybe Mrs. Seales is going to tell me something wise, but just then one kid bops another on the head with a plastic sand bucket and she goes over to help the two of them make peace.

On Saturday, after Cheyenne and Kevin wake up from their naps, Daphne and I put them in strollers and walk them to the park. We spread a blanket on the grass and watch the kids run, free and wild, over to the teeter-totters.

"Grass and trees," I point out. "I didn't even realize I was missing them until we got here."

"Yeah, all that sand and cactus gets boring after a while," Daphne says. "This place is not like Palm Springs, where they've got all those developments with perfect green grass and shade trees and water sprinklers running all the time."

"I've never been to Palm Springs," I tell her.

"We should talk to Vicki, she might take us there sometime before I move. Some of the big hotels are really beautiful, and a lot of movie stars hang out there, especially the old ones."

It seems as if I've looked away from the kids for just a second, but when I look back at the teeter-totter, only Kevin is there. I scan the area, but can't see Cheyenne.

"Did you see where Cheyenne went?" I ask Daphne, my heart pounding in my chest.

"No. She was right there," she says.

Already I am on my feet, running to Kevin.

"Where's Cheyenne?" I yell at him.

He looks at me, blankly, then shrugs his shoulders.

"Cheyenne!" I call.

Daphne is running behind me.

"Look over there," I tell her. "I'll take this side."

I run past the playground, past the picnic tables, thinking of kidnappers and child rapists, vicious dogs and rattlesnakes. I get a glimpse of yellow on the other side of a handball backboard.

"Cheyenne!" I call again, running to the backboard. Relief floods through me when I finally see her, short chubby legs going as fast as they can. Again I call to her, but she doesn't turn back. I catch up with her and pick her up.

"Down!" she says. "Daddy!" she points in the direction of a group of three guys sitting near a barbecue pit. One of them is wearing a black and silver Raiders T-shirt, just like Rudy's.

"Come on, let's go back and play with Kevin," I say.

"Daddy!" she says. "I want Daddy!"

I walk over closer to the men. "Look, Cheyenne. That's not Daddy, it's just someone in the same kind of shirt."

Just then the man stands, showing a big belly.

"See, Sweetheart," I say.

She clings to me, face up against my neck, so I feel her tears. "Daddy," she whispers. "Miss him."

I take her back to the swings and push her for what seems like hours. She doesn't cry any more, or ask about Rudy, but she is very quiet for the rest of the day. How is all this affecting her, I wonder.

On Thursday, my birthday, it's just an ordinary day. I write in my journal first thing in the morning. I'm feeling better about my journal now, partly because in the *Go Ask Alice* book, that girl writes in a diary and it seems to help her figure things out. I've got plenty to figure out, so maybe it's helping me, too.

Today, the questions are: What is important to you? If you could create something beautiful, what would it be?

These are hard questions for me. Cheyenne is important to me. And I want to live a good life. I want to be happy. But how? As far as creating something beautiful, I've already done that with Cheyenne. But I can't paint a beautiful picture because I'm no good at all at art. I'd like to create beautiful music, like the guy in that movie "Amadeus." But I don't know anything about music and I can't sing at all, except to Cheyenne. She likes my singing but I don't think anyone else does.

If I were still at Hamilton High, at that Infant Center, Bergie and the other moms there would have a little party for me. We always do that when it's someone's birthday. But I guess they don't do that at Desert Dunes. Either that or Mrs. Seales hasn't checked my records to see what my birthdate is.

I'll admit that by the end of the day I'm feeling kind of sorry for myself. It *is* my eighteenth birthday, after all, the day that was supposed to be my wedding day. Not that I've ever had a real birthday party or anything. But my mom usually sends me a card. And Rudy gave me some cologne last year, and Irma baked a cake for me. She was all out of candles, but still, it was a cake, and they knew it was my birthday. Here, no one even knows. I guess if I weren't so shy I'd tell people, but that wouldn't be like me at all.

I remember a song my mom used to always listen to — a classic, she claimed. It started out "I've got a feeling called the blue-oo-oo-oo-oos since my baby went away. Lord I don't know what to do-oo-oo-oo . . . " I always thought it was kind of a stupid song, even if it was a classic. But it makes sense to me today because that's how I'm feeling — blue-oo-oo-oo.

After dinner though, just when I'm feeling totally sorry for myself, I notice Daphne and Patricia exchange sly looks. They leave the table. Carla gets up, turns out the kitchen light, and sits back down. Then Daphne and Patricia come back with a cake, eighteen candles lit, and place it in front of me.

"Happy birthday to you," they sing. "Happy birthday to you."

I start laughing and crying all at the same time.

"Don't go getting sentimental on us," Daphne says.

"Make a wish!" Carla says.

I watch the candles burn lower, not even able to figure out what to wish for."

"C'mon," Alice says. "We don't want wax on our icing!"

"Just like Alice to worry about *her* piece of cake on *your* birthday," Patricia says. Everyone laughs.

"Well, damn it! If I don't worry about me who will?" Alice says.

I blow out the candles. I just wish things could be better. That's all I know to wish for.

The cake is chocolate. My favorite. Daphne is smiling a big, happy smile.

"Thanks," I say.

"Patricia helped," Daphne says.

"Thanks, everybody," I say, cutting the cake and passing pieces around.

Daphne comes around with vanilla ice cream and puts a scoop on each dish. I try to help Cheyenne eat her ice cream and cake, but she reaches for the spoon.

"Baby help!" she says.

"Baby help," I laugh, handing her the spoon and watching her get ice cream not only in her mouth, but in her hair, on her hands, and all over the high chair tray.

When Cheyenne's finished, I thank everyone for making my birthday a special day, then take my sticky daughter directly to the bathtub. I wash her hair with baby shampoo, and play hide the ducky with her, then sit and watch her play. She likes to spend about an hour in the bathtub, which is fine with me, as long as no one else is waiting for their turn. She washes the ducky's face and back while I think of how different this birthday was supposed to be.

For a moment, I imagine being in Las Vegas, with Rudy, getting married in a little chapel with wedding bells, like I've seen on TV. We would have been happy today.

But . . . I turn my thoughts to a different day. "I'll tell you what to do, bitch! And you better do it!" And then, I hear the slap, remember the pain, hear "Stop with that goddamned baby help crap," hear Cheyenne's cry, and know what would have come after my Las Vegas birthday. Not that day, maybe, or the next, but it would have come.

Wouldn't it?

There's a knock at the door.

"Can we come in?" Daphne says.

"Sure." I pull the plug so the water will drain from the tub.

"No, Mommy!" Cheyenne says.

"Yes," I tell her. "It's Kevin's turn now."

Daphne comes in with Keven wrapped in a towel.

"My turn," he says, looking down at Cheyenne who is trying to float the ducky in about half an inch of water.

"C'mon, kiddo," I say, wrapping the towel around her and lifting her from the tub.

Daphne refills it, places Kevin in it, and sits on the edge. I sit on the closed toilet, drying Cheyenne.

"It was really nice of you to do the cake for me."

"It was fun. You should have seen your face! You were so surprised."

Cheyenne spreads her towel down on the floor and hands me a diaper from the stack I keep in the bathroom. After I fasten her diaper, she stands up and reaches into the tub for the ducky. Kevin grabs it and swishes it around, making quacking noises. Cheyenne joins in and she and Kevin get us laughing so hard tears roll down our faces. Daphne doubles over with laughter — not that funny little laugh she usually has but a big, loud stream of laughter. I don't know what's so funny about two little kids making quacking noises, but it sure got us laughing.

When we calm down Daphne tells me, "I wish we could leave here at the same time and go to a halfway house together."

"Couldn't you just stay a few extra weeks, until it's time for me to leave?" I ask.

"They're strict about that," she says, shaking her head sadly. "I feel like we're already good friends, just in this short time. I don't want to lose touch with you."

"I know. Usually I'm afraid to make friends, because I know I'll be moving on anyway. But with you it was like we just started out being friends. We didn't even have to try."

Suddenly I feel lonely, realizing how much I like Daphne and Kevin, and how they'll soon be leaving.

"Maybe Cheyenne and I could leave when you do," I say.

"You have to be here six weeks or you won't qualify for a halfway house."

Neither of us says anything for a few minutes, then Daphne says, "We just have to be careful to write and call each other."

I nod, thinking how when I was younger I would have a pact with a friend to always keep in touch, and then something would happen, an address lost, a phone disconnected, something. I'll try to make things be different with Daphne, and I know she'll try, too, but my strongest feeling is that I'll soon be losing a friend.

That night I lay awake for a long time thinking, hearing the occasional sound of a car in the distance, aware of Cheyenne's peaceful breathing. Then, not long after I finally drop off to sleep, sometime early in the morning, Cheyenne wakes crying. I rush to her.

"Shhh, Baby, it's okay, Mommy's here."

"Mommy! Mommy!" she cries.

Her diaper's okay. She's not feverish. A bad dream?

"Mommy!" she shrieks.

"Shhh, shhh," I say, picking her up and holding her close to me.

I rock back and forth with her, trying to soothe her, but she keeps crying. Finally, not knowing what else to do, I carry her from the bedroom, down the hall, and out to the play yard. We sit on the swing and sway gently. Slowly, her sobbing stops.

"Look at the moon, Baby."

"Wow!" she says.

"I see the moon, the moon sees me. God bless the moon, and God bless me," I sing, not knowing where I learned the song.

"Wow" is right. One thing about this sandy old desert I could get used to is the night sky. The moon and stars are bright and shining out here, not filtered by smog, or dulled by city lights.

Tonight, the moon is nearly full, dazzling.

"Put your head down on my shoulder," I tell Cheyenne.

She is asleep in an instant, but I still glide back and forth on the swing drinking in the moon and stars. I remember when I first learned that men had walked on the moon. When I told my mom I wanted to walk on the moon, too, she said, "Yeah, and I wanna be Queen of England." Well, that's my mom. She never hit me though, that's one thing I'll say for her.

My mom might be looking up at the sky right now. It's possible. She always stays up late. Maybe right now she's looking at the sky and remembering how I wanted to walk on the moon. Or maybe she's remembering how she once read *Goodnight, Moon* to Cheyenne.

Who else is looking up at this amazing sky? Maybe Rudy is looking at the moon and wondering how it looks in Las Vegas. Or Sean. Maybe he's in the mountains somewhere, in the Conservation Corps, looking up through pine trees and remembering the full moon over the ocean the night we sat in the sand and talked until the sun came up. Or even, maybe Bergie couldn't sleep tonight, and she's looking up at the moon and thinking about all the kids and the moms at the Infant Care Center. And maybe, for just a minute, she misses us.

Is it possible that someone, somewhere, is looking up at this bright, shining moon and thinking of me? Of us? We are so alone. I want so much for us to belong somewhere, with someone, but where? Who?

7

The kids at Desert Dunes are friendly, teachers are nice, but I keep my distance. I'll be leaving again in a few weeks.

Cheyenne doesn't know yet how that works. Until now, she's known the same people all her life — me, Rudy, Irma, the same kids at the Hamilton High Infant Center. She goes to the new Infant Center as eager to play with Eric and Tyler and Nora as if they'll be her lifelong friends.

I'm not sure if she misses Ethan and Brittany or not. I didn't know she missed Rudy until that day at the park. That's the thing with two-year-olds. It's hard to know what they're feeling inside.

At school, after my last class and before I'm scheduled to work in the Infant Center, I stop at the pay phone. I try to reach my mom, but the number I got from her a few weeks ago has been disconnected.

I don't know what makes me do it, but I call Rudy's house. Like maybe I'll just hear someone's voice and hang up, but when Irma answers, I answer back.

"Melissa! Where are you? Is Cheyenne okay? We've been worried to death!"

I can feel the intensity in her voice.

"We're fine."

"Tell me where you are and I'll come get you!"

"I'm in a safe place. I just wanted to tell you we're okay," I say.

"Please. Come home. Rudy's crazy without you — doesn't eat, can't sleep. Please, come home. Please."

She is crying, pleading, when suddenly all of her sadness turns to anger.

"We have a right to see Cheyenne! She's ours too, you know!"

I can't talk. I only listen.

"At least give me your phone number," she demands.

"I'll call again," I say, and hang up.

The metal side of the phone enclosure is cool against my forehead. I keep asking myself, why did I do it? What did I expect?

I stand straight and take five deep, cleansing breaths, the way we do at the beginning and end of each group meeting at the shelter.

"Hey, how 'bout letting someone else use the phone?"

It's a guy from my English class.

I take one more deep breath, then walk over to the Infant Center, where I wash my hands thoroughly, put on a clean apron, and check to see what needs to be done. Cheyenne is napping, her wrist resting lightly on her mouth. Some babies suck their thumbs, but mine sucks her wrist. Just looking at her makes my heart smile.

Two boys are fighting over a fire truck.

"Anthony's been cross all day," Mrs. Seales tells me. "Why don't you read to him for a while?"

I find Anthony's favorite book, *Machines at Work*, and sit down beside him. He immediately lets go of the fire truck and turns his attention to the picture of a big bulldozer.

It's good to be with little kids because they need so much attention. That way I can't pay attention to my own problems. Time out from problems. I get that from being with little kids, and from reading books. Maybe that's the answer to a journal question I left blank last week — what steps can you take to minimize the feelings of stress and anxiety which may sometimes seem overwhelming?

A few mornings before Daphne and Kevin are scheduled to leave, I see her in the rec room, with her pictures, crying. I sit down beside her. She has the happy family, christening day picture in one hand, and the picture of her nude, brutally battered and bruised, in the other hand.

"Daphne?"

She looks up at me, wiping her eyes.

"I don't know which is real," she says.

"They're both real," I say.

"Sometimes I miss this one so much."

She holds up the happy family picture.

"But this . . . "

"We need more pictures," I tell her.

On the way back from school Cheyenne and I stop at a drugstore to get diapers and I buy one of those box camera things — disposable, like the diapers.

Daphne and I take the kids to the park for pictures.

"Photo opportunities," Daphne laughs, aiming the camera at me, Cheyenne, and Kevin lined up on the ladder to the slide. Daphne and I trade places and I take her picture with the kids. We pretend to be professional photographers, posing each other, talking with fake accents.

"Zee light ees not right," Daphne says, and then we crack up.

"Zee nose casts a shadow," I tell her, turning her head slightly and snapping a picture.

We fall back on the grass, laughing, and Cheyenne and Kevin throw themselves on top of us. We roll around on the grass, like I've seen wild animals do on those TV nature programs.

Later, when the kids are on the climbing structure, Daphne and I sit on a bench, watching them.

An older woman sits on a bench nearby. Her hair is tied back in a red bandanna. I wonder if she knows she's wearing gang colors. She's throwing scraps of bread from a plastic bag onto the grass around her. Pigeons gather, pecking quickly at the crumbs.

"Gone!" she says, emptying the last of the bread onto the ground and shaking out the bag.

"See you tomorrow!" she says, waving her arms at the pigeons.

She seems like such a nice person, it's easy for me to walk over to her and ask if she'd be willing to take a picture of me and Daphne together.

"I'll do my best," she says.

I hand her the camera and call Cheyenne and Kevin down to sit on the bench with us.

"What pretty children you all are," the woman says, then snaps the picture. "Children of the creator, just like my pigeons, and all my kitty cats at home."

She hands the camera back to me, shakes hands with Cheyenne and Kevin, and walks away. The kids go back to the climbing structure and Daphne and I sit with our faces turned toward the gentle late afternoon sun, our eyes on our cubs.

"This is a freedom time," Daphne says.

"What do you mean?"

"Sometimes, not very often, but sometimes, I feel free. Like today. Nothing will hurt me today, and I can say whatever I want, and be silly if I want, and no one will hit me, or be mean. I want all my times to be freedom times."

By the time I get the pictures developed, Daphne and Kevin have already gone on to a halfway house somewhere in Upland. The pictures make me laugh, but I'm left feeling lonely for my friend. It's not that I don't like anyone else here. I do, but there's no one I feel close to, the way I felt close to Daphne.

I divide the pictures, being careful to put two of the best ones in the pile for Daphne. When I come to the one of the four of us, I can't decide who should get that picture. I wish we'd had the bird lady take two pictures of us that day. Why didn't I think of that?

Finally, the picture of the four of us goes into Daphne's pile. She needs the best pictures possible to balance out the awful pictures she already has in her collection.

I put the pictures in an envelope with her name on it and a note that says, "Remember the freedom time? I miss you, and Cheyenne asks about Kevin every morning as soon as she wakes up."

Vickie will take the pictures over to the halfway house next week. I wish I could call Daphne, but it's still all confidential where she's staying. I hope she'll send me a note back by way of Vickie.

In group we talk of our past, and how to get strong. Alice tells a whole stream of brutal stories.

"One night he came in from the garage where he'd been working on his car. I hadn't finished washing the dishes. Kamille was sitting at the kitchen table with me, doing her homework. You know, one of those first grade things where you circle the right answer in red.

"Anyway, he came in and went crazy because the dishes weren't done. He grabbed me up from the table and slammed me against the wall. He kept banging my head against the wall, calling me every rotten name he could think of. Kamille came running to stand between us, pushing at him, crying. He smacked her, too, the bastard."

Alice's face is shimmering wet with tears. Trish pulls a chair up right next to her and rubs her back. One after another of the women tell stories of being beaten, raped, humiliated in every imaginable way. I start thinking of all the things Rudy *didn't* do. He didn't rape me. He didn't choke me. He didn't kick me. He didn't call me the "C" word. He didn't hit Cheyenne. He was a little rough with her, but he didn't hit her.

"Melissa?"

It is Carla. Everyone's looking at me.

"Are you with us?"

"I was just thinking," I say.

"About?"

"About how I maybe don't belong here."

"Why wouldn't you?" Carla asks.

"Well . . . nothing so bad ever happened to me."

"So are you saying you weren't abused?"

"Well . . . "

Trish turns to me. "Didn't you say your boyfriend hit you?"

"Yes, but not like Alice is talking about," I say, looking at Alice slumped down in her chair, tears still running down her cheeks.

"And called you names," Carla says.

"Yes, but not very often."

"And kept you from seeing friends, or going places."

"Yes, but . . . "

Alice sits straight upright.

"You stupid bi . . . witch," she says. "Don't you know nothing? Abuse is abuse. Maybe my ol' man hit me harder, or yelled louder, but your guy'd catch up eventually. Don't sit there makin' excuses for him.'"

Carla hands me a pamphlet, "It Shouldn't Hurt to Go Home."

"I know you've got one of these in the packet of things I gave you when you first got here, but do me a favor and take a look again. Check off the things that apply to your Rudy."

There's a whole list of categories, with explanations. The first is "Physical Abuse" and it talks about hitting, slapping, kicking, choking, pushing, punching, beating. I guess I can put a check mark beside that one.

"Verbal abuse." Constant criticism, humiliating remarks, not responding to what the victim is saying, mocking, name-calling, yelling, swearing, interrupting, changing the subject. Check.

"Sexual violence." Forcing sex, demanding sexual acts that the victim does not want to perform, degrading treatment. No check on this one.

"Isolation." Making it hard to see friends, monitoring phone calls, controlling where the victim goes. Check, I guess, if I think about Sean, and how I always had to stay home in case Rudy would call from work.

There's more to the list, but that's already enough to make me face the fact that yes, Rudy was abusing me.

"Just because others have been more badly beaten doesn't excuse what Rudy's done, does it?"

I shake my head. "It's just that sometimes, when I remember the good things, I get all confused."

There is a kind of cynical laughter from the group.

"Here's the thing," Trish says. "When you remember the good times, keep remembering. Pretty soon you'll get to a bad time and you won't be confused anymore. You belong here just as much as any of the rest of us."

I nod, but inside I'm not sure I believe it. Belong. Belong. I don't even know for sure what that means. It's weird, how that girl in the book I've been reading belonged to a totally loving family, grandparents and all, and she still messed up big time. I think if I had a family like hers, life would be so much better for me. Really, I don't think that book is going to end up being one of my best friends. It makes me mad, the way that girl uses drugs and hurts her family. I feel sorry for her and all, especially because she dies so young, but I don't respect her the way I do Scout, in *To Kill a Mockingbird,* or Margaret, in that Judy Blume book.

It is the Sunday before we're scheduled to leave for a half-way house placement. One more week at Desert Dunes High School, and we'll move on again. I was hoping we'd end up in the same halfway house as Daphne and Kevin, but there's no room there. The place we're going is down near San Diego. If we're there long enough, maybe we'll see my mom when she works the Del Mar racing season. Alice and Kamille are already at the San Diego place. Of all people to end up with, Alice is about last on my list. She's okay, I guess, but she can be hard to get along with.

What's going to happen there is we'll figure out how to live on our own. How to find a job, and take care of basic bills, that kind of thing. I hate to move Cheyenne again. She seems sort of withdrawn sometimes now. Like maybe she's learning what I already know, that you can't have special friends for long if you're constantly on the move. Oh, well. One day at a time, as Trish is always saying.

I don't exactly believe it though. This girl that I'm reading about takes one day at a time and her life gets messed up big time. She's lots worse off than I am because of the drugs. I've never done drugs and I'm sure not going to start now. In my opinion that's one of the worst things a mom can do — be a druggie or a drunk.

I'm bored. My homework is done. I've written in my journal. I miss Daphne. There's no one here to laugh with.

"Come on, Cheyenne," I say, picking her up from where she sits playing with blocks."Let's go for a walk."

"Walk! Wow!" she says.

I put her in the stroller and fasten the belt.

"We'll be back in an hour or so," I tell Trish.

I guess we'll go to the park, but that doesn't sound like much fun without Daphne and Kevin. Where else, though? The library's closed. Cheyenne could use some new shoes, but I don't have much money so it would only be frustrating to go shopping.

A block from the park I hear a car with a noisy muffler. Cheyenne and I both turn to look. I catch my breath at the sight of a gray Ford.

"Daddy's car!" Cheyenne yells, excited, smiling.

For an instant I think it *is* Rudy, but see that the Ford is older, the driver is younger and darker.

"Wow! Daddy!" Cheyenne yells again.

As the car drives past us down the street and out of sight at the curve in the road, Cheyenne's smile fades.

"Daddy?" she says, looking back at me.

"Daddy?" she says again, tears gathering in her deep blue eyes.

I pick her up out of the stroller and hold her close to me.

"That wasn't Daddy. That was someone else."

"Miss him," she says. "Gramma?" she says.

"Gramma's not here, either," I say.

"Miss her," Cheyenne says.

At the park I sit on the bench where Daphne and I sat on the day of our freedom time. It doesn't feel like such a freedom time today. Two older boys, seven or so, are hogging the climbing structure, blocking Cheyenne's way to the top.

"Mommy!" Cheyenne calls, frustrated.

I don't feel like fighting it.

"Come on, let's go down the slide," I say to her.

"My turn!" she yells, pointing at the top.

The boys keep blocking her way.

I watch, knowing it would be a betrayal not to help her out. Reluctantly I get up and walk to the structure, looking up, hoping the boys will get the message. They don't. They just sit stubbornly at the top. I climb up, until I am eye to eye with the biggest boy.

"It's *her* turn," I say.

"We were here first," he says.

I look him in the eye. "Move, you spoiled little butt! Now!"

"You can't make me," he says.

I grab him by the wrist, surprised at my anger. I have an urge to yank him down, fling him to the ground. Quickly, I release him. He and his friend clamber down and run to the swings. I watch Cheyenne take the last two steps to the top, then I climb down. The boys watch me from a distance, wary.

There are families here in the park, lots of children with moms and dads, grandmas and grandpas, uncles, cousins, aunts, and then there is me and Cheyenne. Just the two of us, alone.

I get Cheyenne and go to the pay phone. If it is Rudy, I'll hang up. Irma answers.

"Do you still want to come get us?" I ask.

"Melissa!" she says. "How's the baby?"

"She's fine. Here, talk to her."

I put the phone to Cheyenne's ear.

"Say hello," I urge her.

"Yo," she says.

"Hello, Cheyenne, oh, my baby," Irma says.

"Gramma!" Cheyenne yells, smiling a huge smile.

I take the phone back.

"Irma?"

"Tell me where, I'll leave right now. God, I'm so relieved to know Cheyenne is safe."

Irma is crying, but sort of laughing, too. I notice it is Cheyenne she's been worried about, not me. Oh, well, at least Cheyenne has a gramma who loves her.

"I'm not sure how you should get here. It's Desert Dunes."

"Give me cross streets, I'll look it up on the map."

I tell her the two streets. "And it's Prospector's Park," I say.

"I'll be there. Probably in an hour and a half, I'm not sure how long it'll take, but I'm leaving."

"Will you bring the carseat?"

"Yes. I'll get it from the garage."

We always kept the car seat in Rudy's car. It's funny to think of it sitting unused in the dusty garage.

"Don't tell Rudy you're coming for me," I say.

"He's not here right now," Irma says. "He'll be home later."

Back at the shelter I get our things out of the stroller and repack important items in our backpacks — as many items of clothing as I can stuff in, plus my journal. As much as I didn't like writing in my journal in the beginning, now it's like a friend to me. I want to keep writing in it because it helps me think things through.

I go into the empty office and get my papers from the file cabinet, then write a note for Carla, thanking her, telling her I can't exactly explain it but I've got to go back home for a while. I seal the envelope and put it on the dresser where I know it will be found. When I don't show up for dinner tonight they'll probably look in our room.

"We're going back down to the park," I say to Trish on our way out.

"Don't you want the stroller?" she asks.

"We'll just walk this time," I say.

Trish looks at me rather suspiciously, but says nothing more. At dinner tonight I will be a topic of conversation. Trish may mention she thought something was funny when I didn't take the stroller. And then they'll find the note.

Maybe I'm wrong to go back, but I'm just not up for the halfway house, another group of strangers, and watching Cheyenne get her hopes up that the next gray car is her dad's, the next chunky woman is her gramma.

It is nearly dark when I see Irma's burgundy Honda slow down in front of the park. Cheyenne and I take off, waving, our backpacks bumping up and down as we run. Irma spots us, stops the car, and gets out.

"Cheyenne!" she calls.

"Gramma!"

Cheyenne runs faster, full force, into Irma's outstretched arms.

"My baby," Irma says, laughing and crying at the same time. She picks Cheyenne up and carries her to the car. I follow behind, aware that Irma has not greeted *me* so warmly. In fact, she's not greeted me at all.

8

As usual, Cheyenne is asleep in her carseat by the time we've driven two miles.

"You called just in time, Melissa. I was getting ready to file a kidnapping report against you."

"What do you mean, kidnapping?"

"You know. Kidnapping. And child endangerment, too. I was just waiting for my next paycheck so I could get a lawyer to file charges."

It is as if Irma is speaking a foreign language, that's how hard it is for me to understand what she's saying.

"Child endangerment? Cheyenne wasn't in danger."

"That was an awful thing you did, taking the baby away from us. After all I've done for you, too. You'd have been out on the street if it wasn't for me."

Irma reaches across me and gets some tissue from the glove compartment. She dabs at her eyes.

"I'm so disappointed in you. Your own mother didn't want to be bothered with you, and I took you in and then you steal our baby away from us."

"How can I steal my own baby?"

"She's not just *your* baby. Rudy's name's on that birth certificate too, you know."

In the off and on glow of headlights and streetlights, Irma's face looks hard, and set. Even at stoplights she doesn't turn to look at me. I hadn't expected her anger. If *she's* this angry, what will Rudy be like when I see him?

I should reach back and unbuckle Cheyenne — be ready to get out at the next stop light. Run with her back to the shelter. I look around for familiar landmarks. Nothing. We're in the middle of nowhere and I wouldn't even know which direction to run.

We drive for miles, not talking. Irma's got a Mexican station on, with Mariachi music. It's peppy and upbeat, the opposite of how I'm feeling.

By the time we get to Pomona, things are looking more familiar. It is late, and for once the freeway is not all jammed up. My stomach is growling from hunger. I wish I had at least thought to put a couple of apples in my backpack.

Irma sighs and turns off the radio.

"You know, Rudy lost his job because of you."

I stare out the window, wondering what's going to come next.

"Mr. Murphy was using Rudy every day on that remodeling job, even giving him overtime, but Rudy was so stressed out over you kidnapping Cheyenne that he just lost it."

"I *didn't* kidnap my own baby! I took her to a safe place!"

"Well, all I know's Rudy's out of work and it never would have happened if you hadn't run off with the baby."

"So Rudy lost his temper and did something stupid and you're blaming it on me?"

"I know my son! He doesn't just go around throwing hammers through windows for no good reason!"

Irma wipes tears of anger from her cheeks, still keeping her eyes on the road ahead. It's weird. I never had hopes that Irma would love me like a daughter, or any of that fairytale stuff, but I never thought she'd hate me. Now, it's like she hates me.

"If Rudy threw a hammer through a window it's because he decided to do that, not because I made him."

"Oh, I suppose that's going to be your attitude now. You're not responsible for anything," she says, oozing sarcasm. "Rudy's been sick with worry over you. Carrying your picture wherever he goes, driving around at all hours, asking strangers on the street if they've seen you . . . "

Irma turns off the freeway and into familiar territory. I can see the tower of Hamilton High School from here and I realize with a jolt how much I've missed this familiar school and all that goes with it — friends, classes, teachers, the Infant Center.

"Rudy's been so upset over you leaving — you've made him crazy."

"I'm responsible for my own behavior, not Rudy's," I say.

Irma lets out a snort of derision. "You've picked up so much bull shit along the way you smell like a cow pasture."

I won't cry. I won't cry. Over and over again I think those words. I take deep, cleansing breaths, the way I learned to do at the shelter. How stupid I was to call Irma.

"You have a little tiff and you go running off to some home for battered women. You girls today are so spoiled! Let me tell you, I didn't go running off with Rudy every time his father got a little mad on. I minded my mouth and stuck it out. Children belong with their fathers just as much as they do with their mothers."

"Well, that's why I'm coming back," I say.

"I didn't want to take a baby on, at my age," Irma says, again dabbing at tears. "But Rudy insisted and then, I loved her so much, that sweet little thing . . . " she is crying full out now, and I worry that she can't see where she's going.

"Then you took her away from me, with no warning . . . "

"We're back, Irma. We're back," I say, trying to be as reassuring as possible.

"But I don't trust you anymore. The least little thing'll come up and who knows what you'll do . . . "

Rudy is sitting on the front porch, smoking, when we drive into the driveway. Even in the dark I can see his wide smile. He runs to the car and opens my door, taking me by the hand and guiding me out. He is laughing.

"I knew you'd come back. I kept telling Mom, she'll be back, just wait."

He gives me a big hug and says he's missed me. Then he opens the back door and gently gets Cheyenne from her carseat. She stirs.

"Hi, Baby," he whispers.

She opens her eyes wide. "Daddy!" she shrieks. "Daddy!"

We all laugh, even Irma. Rudy carries her and her backpack into the house and Irma and I follow.

"Phew!" he says, laughing.

Rudy puts her down on the couch and gets a diaper and baby wipes from her backpack. He cleans her up and kisses her belly, then he puts a fresh diaper on her. He puts her on the floor and she takes off running into the room where we kept all her toys.

"Mary!" she says, carrying her baby doll out to show me.

"Mary missed you," Rudy says.

"Miss 'em," Cheyenne says, walking into the kitchen.

It's as if she has to check out every nook and cranny, looking for familiar things.

Now that we're in the house, Irma's face has lost the hard, stony look she had in the car. She sits in the recliner, feet up.

"What a long drive," she says.

"Well, it's over now," Rudy says, smiling at me. "It's all over now."

I feel an old warmth rushing through me as I see Rudy's glowing smile and the tender look in his eyes. Maybe everything's going to work out.

"Come to Gramma," Irma says, reaching toward Cheyenne.

Irma helps Cheyenne climb into the chair. She kisses the top of Cheyenne's head.

"Your hair smells good," Irma says.

Well, I think, at least she knows I've been keeping Cheyenne clean. And one look at her chubby little body and anyone can tell she's been well fed. Child endangerment! What a stupid idea!

My stomach growls again, so loud Cheyenne laughs and points to me. I'm starving, but I can't bring myself to say so. And in spite of the growls, neither Irma nor Rudy offer anything to eat. Well, I can wait until morning. It won't kill me.

Cheyenne is not so shy about asking for food. She points in the direction of the kitchen.

"Juice. Cracker," she says.

Irma gets up and goes to the kitchen. She puts Cheyenne in her high chair and gives her juice and crackers. I get a container of bananas and cereal and bring it into the kitchen. Irma watches while I feed Cheyenne, then says goodnight.

Rudy runs bath water and together we bathe Cheyenne. It's nice to be where she has her own clothes. She laughs when she sees her favorite Minnie Mouse pajamas.

Cheyenne clutches Mary in one hand, sucks the wrist of her other hand, and is fast on her way to sleeping by the time we walk out the bedroom door. I can tell she is happy to be in her own crib, with her own bird mobile.

Rudy sits on the couch in the living room, his arm resting on the back, as if expecting me to nestle in beside him. I sit in Irma's recliner, flipping through an old magazine, feeling awkward now that we are alone. Where will I sleep? How will things be? Will I ever be comfortable enough here to go to the refrigerator and help myself to something to eat?

It is so quiet in here I can hear Rudy take a deep breath, then sigh. I glance up from the magazine I'm pretending to read. He is leaning forward, looking at me, eyebrows raised, as if he's expecting me to say something, or do something. I look back at the magazine and turn another page.

"Missy," he says, in a whisper.

I close the magazine and look up.

"Come sit by me."

We watch each other, neither of us moving. The air between us seems heavy, almost solid.

"Please," he says, patting the couch on the cushion beside him.

I walk through the heavy air and sit beside him, breathing in his familiar scent of soap and cigarettes.

"I love you," he says.

His words, his presence, draw me to him with a force stronger than caution. He holds me tight, whispering.

"I didn't know how much I needed you 'til you were gone. Stay with me, Missy, don't leave me again. I won't hurt you, I swear, I'll only love you. I learned my lesson. I learned my lesson."

It is as though somewhere deep within me a dam bursts, releasing floods of sorrow and loneliness. Shaking and sobbing, I bury my face in Rudy's chest.

"Hold me," I say. "Don't let me go."

"No, never," he promises, and I know that all of my questions about belonging are answered. I belong with Rudy, wherever he is, that's where I belong. Rudy and I, and Cheyenne — a family of people who belong together.

Rudy stands and pulls me to him, kissing me tenderly on the lips. He takes my hand and leads me into his bedroom where Cheyenne sleeps soundly in her crib, still clutching Mary. He pulls me to him again. This time his kisses are more insistent. He pulls my sweater up and puts his hand inside my bra. I cling to him, wanting to get closer, to lose myself in this moment.

We move to the bed, grappling with buttons and zippers until I feel Rudy, hard, pressing between my legs.

For a fleeting instant I wonder if a week off the pill means I could get pregnant, then I open to Rudy, taking him in, thinking nothing else, feeling nothing else, only Rudy. Rudy. Rudy.

Cheyenne wakes at six-thirty, smiling over her crib at us.

"Baby help," she says.

I get out of bed and let down the crib side, so Cheyenne can climb out by herself. She struggles, trying to do it all one-handed while she keeps a hold on her doll.

"Here, let me hold Mary for you," I tell her.

She pauses, then hands the doll to me, grips the crib railing with both hands and climbs over. She runs to the bed where Rudy still sleeps, covers pulled over his head. She pulls the covers away from his face and pokes at his eyes.

"Daddy. Wake."

"No," he says, then pretends to snore.

"Wake!" she says, trying to force his eyelids open.

In one quick move he swoops her into bed with him.

"I'm gonna eat you up," he says, making gobbling sounds and munching gently at her.

Cheyenne laughs like I've not heard her laugh in weeks.

Irma knocks on the door and comes walking in.

"Hungry, Baby?" she says, smiling at Cheyenne.

"Go with Gramma before I eat you all, all up," Rudy says, lifting Cheyenne and holding her out to Irma.

"I need to leave in about fifteen minutes," Irma says, carrying Cheyenne out of the room.

As soon as they're gone, Rudy gives me a sly grin.

"Fifteen minutes is plenty of time," he says.

I quick close the door and crawl back in bed.

"Quiet, though," I whisper.

"As a mouse," he says, taking my hand and guiding it to him.

After Irma leaves for work we get up and fix a huge breakfast, bacon, eggs, orange juice, and a kind of cinnamon toast that's sort of Rudy's specialty.

"How long's it been since you've eaten?" Rudy says, watching me wolf down food.

I smile, embarrassed, and slow down.

Cheyenne sits in her high chair and Rudy feeds her little bites of scrambled egg in between his own big bites. Watching them, I'm as happy as I've ever been. This is what I want, right here, not some halfway house with a bunch of women I don't even know — complaining women at that.

We clean up the kitchen and get Cheyenne dressed. Rudy sings silly made-up songs to Cheyenne, and every time I look his way he's got this big smile on his face. Same for me. I can't stop smiling, either.

"I should go get set up with classes this afternoon," I tell him.

His smile fades. "Why don't we spend today together, just the three of us. It's been so long."

"Well, okay. I don't want to miss much school, though."

"Just today," he says, putting his arms around me. "Huh, Cheyenne," he says. "Just today."

"Today!" she repeats, causing us both to laugh.

We spend the day talking about how things are going to be. For sure we're going to Vegas to get married just as soon as we can. And Rudy's going to get another job, better than the last one.

"Ol' Murphy didn't know his ass from a hole in the ground," Rudy says.

"I thought you liked him?"

Rudy's face clouds over.

"That's before I saw what an asshole he is."

"What happened?" I ask.

"Nothin'. It's over. I don't want to talk about it."

Rudy walks out the back door and sits on the steps, smoking. I gather up dirty clothes and put a load in the washer, then Cheyenne and I vacuum. She loves to push the vacuum cleaner.

I think if Irma comes home to a clean house, maybe she'll start to like me again. Or at least stop hating me.

After we finish vacuuming we take Cheyenne's big plastic ball outside and bounce it back and forth. Rudy plays, too. His smile is back. When Cheyenne tires of the game, Rudy and I sit on the steps and watch while she goes from flower to flower, sticking her nose into each one, then looking at us and smiling.

"Yum, yum," she says at each stop.

I go inside and get the pictures Daphne and I took at the park, then sit back down beside Rudy.

"Look, this is my friend from the desert," I say, pointing to Daphne.

He glances at the picture, then looks away.

"And this is her little boy, Kevin."

This time he doesn't even look.

"That's over, Missy. I don't want you even thinking about it."

I tuck the pictures back in my pocket and move closer to Rudy, not wanting to spoil things.

When Cheyenne starts showing signs of sleepiness we put her down for a nap, and again we make quick, quiet, love. It's like we can't get enough of each other.

Later in the afternoon, I call for an appointment with Planned Parenthood. When I was in the desert I didn't know where to go to get a refill on my birth control pills. The woman I talk with there tells me we should be using condoms until I complete a new, full month's cycle.

I hope I can explain it to Rudy. Why should that be a problem? We do the most private, intimate things with our bodies, but then I can hardly get up enough nerve to talk about something as simple as using a condom.

By the time Irma gets home, at six-fifteen, the house is spotless and dinner is ready. I used the last of my welfare check to buy the makings for spaghetti and garlic bread and brownies. Irma loves brownies.

"How's Gramma's baby?" she asks, and Cheyenne runs to her.

She smiles and says hello to Rudy, and just sort of nods at me.

But I can tell by the way she looks around, she likes what she sees. I'll keep doing my share, more than my share, and Irma'll get over being mad at me — I'm pretty sure.

Late at night, after Cheyenne has been asleep for hours, I tell Rudy, "This was the happiest day of my life."

"Mine, too," he says. "That's how they're all going to be from now on. Happy days."

9

"We want all happy days," Rudy tells me, watching as I get ready for school. "Stay here with me."

"But Rudy, it's already Thursday. I don't want to miss any more school."

"All I'm asking is that you and Cheyenne stay home with me, just 'til I find another job, that's all. Is that too much to ask?"

"No," I say, searching for my old notebook to put into my backpack. "But I don't want to mess up my chances for graduation."

"You care more about your stupid graduation than you do about me and Cheyenne," he says, scowling.

I go to where he's sitting on the edge of the bed and put my arms around him. "That's not true. You're the most important person in my whole life — you and Cheyenne. You know that."

"Stay with me then, just one more day. Tomorrow I'll personally drive you over to Hamilton so you can get started again. Promise."

His deep brown eyes, sincere, pleading, captivate me.

"Okay," I whisper.

"One more happy day," he says with a smile.

I smile back, keeping my uneasiness buried below the surface, thinking how lucky I am that Rudy cares so much, and that he needs me.

Friday morning Rudy insists that Monday is a better day to start.

"Cheyenne needs to get back to preschool, too," I tell him.

"Monday's soon enough," he says.

"When are you going to start looking for another job?" I ask.

"Whenever," he says.

Instead of getting registered at school on Monday, we go to the Department of Social Services, where we wait in one place after the next to get my address changed back to Rudy's house. It was just one check that they sent to the shelter and now it's like a very big deal to send my checks to the same place they've been sending them for over two years.

Cheyenne is tired and fussy, and there's nothing I can do but hold her on my lap while I wait for my number to be called. If I let her go she tries to run out the door. Besides that, there's all kinds of things she could hurt herself on in here — tables and desks with sharp corners, swinging doors, people walking around, not looking where they're going.

I bounce Cheyenne around, try to play patty-cake, but she tries to squirm down.

"Look at that," Rudy says, pointing to two women behind the counter.

They are leaning against the counter, laughing and looking at a stack of snapshots. One of the women is very fat. Her hair and make-up look as if she spent a lot of time getting ready this morning. The other woman, the one with the stack of pictures, is short and skinny and sloppy looking, as if she just rolled out of bed and came to work.

"It's like they don't have a goddamned thing in the world to do. Let us peons wait."

Cheyenne lets out a cry and tries to push herself down. Rudy takes her from me and jostles her up and down.

"I hate that," Rudy tells me. "They think they're so much better than anyone else, with their forms and numbers."

"Maybe it's their break," I say.

"Shit, Missy. They're just letting us know who's boss, that's all. I know about people like that," he says, angrily enough that several people glance up at him.

Cheyenne tries to push away from Rudy.

"No, Cheyenne!" he says, the angry tone still in his voice.

Cheyenne pulls her mouth down into her saddest look, then opens it wide and lets out a shriek.

"Jesus!" Rudy says, shoving Cheyenne back at me.

"Number fifty-seven," the woman who is *not* looking at snapshots calls out.

I look at my number again, even though I know exactly what it says. Eighty-nine.

Cheyenne is crying, full blast, and now everyone's looking at us. What am I supposed to do, anyway? It's like I'm making her cry just to annoy them or something.

"Rudy, maybe you should take Cheyenne for a ride. She's so tired, and I know she'd go to sleep in the carseat."

"What?" he says.

I talk louder, over Cheyenne's crying.

"Take her for a ride so she'll go to sleep," I say.

He walks away, over to the counter in front of where the two women are still talking and looking at pictures.

"Hey!" he says.

Neither of the women responds.

"Hey! Goddammit!"

Now, instead of looking at Cheyenne, everyone's looking at Rudy.

He bangs on the counter. The larger of the two looks up.

"You work here?"

"Please take a number and wait your turn, sir."

"I asked you a question."

The sloppy one nods in the direction of a giant, uniformed security guard, who walks over to the counter, his hand resting on a club that dangles from his belt.

"Peeceman," Cheyenne says, pointing, suddenly happy again.

My throat goes dry and I silently plead for Rudy to calm down, calm down.

"Save your questions for when your number comes up," the woman says. She uses firm, even tones, like teachers do when they're giving one final chance to a difficult child.

The whole room seems to lean toward Rudy, waiting for whatever will come next. Calm down, I'm thinking. Calm down.

"I hope to Christ someday you both have to wait for help from anybody in this room 'cause you won't get it. Flat tire? Mugging? About to drown in a swimming pool? Tough shit, bitches!"

There is a pause in the room and then, as if of one spirit, everyone starts clapping. The security guard has Rudy by the arm, guiding him toward the door, but Rudy manages to turn and flash a Rocky Balboa smile at the crowd. The applause heightens as he is escorted out the door.

The two women look together at the last three pictures, taking their time. Then, finally, the smaller one calls for number fifty-eight. Moments later the larger woman calls for number fifty-nine.

There is a buzz in the room, kind of like at a basketball game after a player's made three free shots in a row.

I hear a tapping at the window and turn to see Rudy motioning to me. He is smiling broadly. Others in the room notice him and they, too, smile. The guard watches, but does not move. I put Cheyenne on the floor, take her by her hand, and the two of us walk to the door. Rudy meets us and picks Cheyenne up. He is laughing.

"How about that?" he says. "I guess we showed those two lazy bitches."

"Bitches," Cheyenne says.

"No, baby," I say.

Rudy puts his hand over his mouth, still laughing, like the whole thing's cute, or something.

"I'll take her for a ride now, get her to sleep," Rudy says.

"Okay. It'll probably be at least another hour."

"See that tree down there?" he says, pointing to a shady place down the block. "After she's asleep real good I'll just wait for you there."

I kiss them both and go back inside. I wish I'd brought a book to read, but I haven't had a chance to get to the library since I left the shelter. In fact, right now is the first time Rudy and I have been apart for over a week.

The only magazines on the table beside me are two ancient issues of *Sports Illustrated* and a beat up *Home Style* from a year ago. I flip through the *Home Style*, wishing it had a story. The pictures are pretty, though, and I can't help wondering what it would be like to live in a great big house with French doors that open onto a deck overlooking the ocean.

There's a picture of a kitchen that's got to be as big as Irma's whole house. I guess there are real people who live in houses like that.

Once, when I was little, Sean's mom, Teresa, drove us around a place called San Marino, so we could see Christmas lights. That place had huge trees, and huge houses, and huge lawns.

"Some people have all the luck," is how Sean's mom explained that we lived in motels near racetracks and other people lived in beautiful, huge houses. Even then, I wondered if it was only luck. I guess it has to be, at least for little kids. Why else was I born to my mom, instead of to some rich mom and dad, where I'd have had my own room, and gone to school with the same kids, year after year?

For that matter, I guess it was luck that got Cheyenne born to me. I hope it was good luck for her, even though we're not in a big house with all matching appliances and she doesn't have her own room with teddy bear curtains and matching lamps. I want to make it be lucky for her, so when she's older and looks around at how everybody else lives, she'll know she got lucky when she got me for a mom.

Why do I cry when I think about this stuff? Cleansing breath, one . . . two . . . three . . . four . . .

"Number eight-nine."

It is the sloppy one calling my number. I put the magazine back and walk quickly to the counter. I explain about the address change. The clerk doesn't look at me or even act as if she's listening. Her whole head disappears as she leans down below the counter. I stand on my tiptoes to try to see what she's doing, but I'm not tall enough to get a good look. When she reappears she slides a form across the counter to me. I wait for an explanation.

"Number ninety," she calls.

"What am I supposed to do about my address change?" I ask.

She looks at me as if I'm the most stupid person she's ever seen.

"Fill this out and mail it in," she says, condescendingly.

"That's all?"

"Fill this out and mail it in," she repeats.

For an instant I'm glad for everything Rudy said to her, and I wish I'd clapped for him, too. Why should we wait over three hours just to pick up a form?

Rudy is still in a good mood when I get to the car.

"Hey, Babe," he says, reaching across the seat and opening the door for me.

Cheyenne is sleeping, her head flopped over to one side. I scrunch up my sweatshirt and prop it into her carseat, so she looks more comfortable.

"Kisses?" Rudy asks.

I kiss him on the cheek and he pulls me closer, kissing me on the mouth. We sit in the car for a while, kissing and hugging, easy at first and then with more intensity, our hands moving to special places, places Rudy's taught me want to be touched.

"Am I your hero?" Rudy whispers to me.

"Mine and everyone else's," I tell him, though I am half-hearted about it.

"Rudy?"

"Yeah, Babes?"

"I want us to go to one of those couples' support groups I've been telling you about."

He backs away, fast. "We don't need that shit," he says.

"For me?" I ask.

"I've got for you," he says, moving close again, nuzzling my neck, making soft animal sounds, making me laugh.

10

"**M**elissa!"

Bergie hurries over to me and gives me a big hug, then reaches for Cheyenne.

"How's my baby-help girl?"

Cheyenne ducks her head shyly, but leans toward Bergie to let her take her from my arms.

Bergie laughs softly and carries her over to the playhouse where Brittany and Ethan are busy playing at the make-believe stove.

"Look who's here," Bergie says, setting Cheyenne down just outside the doorway.

They stop stirring their pretend food and look at Cheyenne. Then Ethan hands her a pan and a spoon. She steps inside the playhouse, and all three of them stir air-food with great enthusiasm.

"How are you?" Bergie asks, turning to me.

I know this is not a question to answer with a quick "Fine, thanks."

"I'm good," I tell her. "Glad to be back."

"How was your time at the shelter?"

"It was okay. I learned a lot. People were good to me, but it wasn't home."

"Are you back at Rudy's?"

"Yes."

Bergie frowns.

"It's okay now," I tell her. "Things are different."

She looks at me with a kind of sad look in her eye.

"Really. Rudy says he knows now how important we are, and that we're only going to have happy days from here on out. Besides, he was never as bad as those guys I heard about at the shelter."

"I hope it works for you, Melissa. For your sake *and* Cheyenne's."

"It will. I just know it. We're getting married as soon as Rudy gets a job."

"I thought he already had a job."

"He got laid off," I say. I guess if I were telling the whole truth I'd probably say he got fired, but I already see more doubt in Bergie's eyes than I want to look at.

My counselor, Ms. Sullivan, says I've been gone too long to get back into all of my old classes. She says I should go to Sojourner Continuation, or to Independent Studies, but I want to stay at Hamilton High and graduate on stage.

"I could catch up, I know I could."

She reviews my records.

"Well, your grades have been good, especially for someone who has the responsibility of a baby."

"Just let me try," I say.

"It's not actually up to me," she says. "You'll have to get permission from your teachers."

She gives me a form to get signed by all of my teachers and tells me to try to catch them between classes, so as not to interrupt them.

First I go to Peer Counseling. I stand at the back, waiting for class to be over so I can talk to Ms. Woods. As usual, everyone's talking at once. The question on the board is "Should gay couples be allowed to attend the prom?"

"Disgusting!" Tony says.

"You're a bigot, Tony," Leticia says.

"Leticia DeLoach," Ms. Woods says, pointing at the NO PUT DOWNS sign.

I'm taking it all in, remembering how much I love this class.

Leticia nods at Ms. Woods. "Okay. But Tony, what I want to know is why do you care about other people's sex lives? They're not trying to get you to change."

"I'm *normal*," Tony says.

"A matter of opinion," Leticia laughs.

Josh turns to say something to Leticia and notices me standing in the back of the room.

"Hey!" he says, smiling.

Leticia walks back to where I'm standing.

"Hey, girlfriend. Where you been? Kidnapped by aliens?"

I laugh, embarrassed by the attention.

Ms. Woods glances at the clock. Only ten minutes left until the bell.

"Come on in and take a seat, Melissa," she says with a smile.

I sit in the back and Leticia sits beside me. Josh is saying he thinks people have a right to behave however they want to, as long as they're not hurting anyone else. Leticia nods in agreement, then turns to me.

"Really, where've you been?" she whispers.

"It's a long story," I say.

"I've got time," she says. "Meet me at lunch."

I feel my face getting warm and I know I'm blushing.

"Just me," she says. "I've got a car today."

"Okay," I tell her. I really like Leticia, but I'm not sure I want to explain the details of running away from Rudy. Now that I'm back, I just want to put the past behind me.

When the bell rings I make my way to Woodsie's desk. I show her the form and ask if it's okay for me to get back into her class.

"Of course," she says. "I'd be delighted to have you back."

She signs the form and hands it back to me.

"Is everything okay with you?"

"It's fine," I say.

She watches, as if waiting for me to say more, but I have nothing else to say.

"Well, I'll see you tomorrow. I'll have a list of back assignments ready for you then."

Before she signs the form, my English teacher, Ms. Lee, goes over what I'll have to do to catch up — lots of reading, two make-up tests, and a compare/contrast paper on two poems by contemporary poets. In the beginning I only signed up for contemporary literature because it was at a convenient time, but it turned out to be a good class. The reading is almost always interesting, so it won't be a problem to do the work. Time is all. It's hard to find time to do everything because of the baby, and housework, and Rudy.

The only teacher who refuses to let me back into class is Mr. Horton, my math teacher.

"You couldn't possibly catch up to what we're doing now. You've missed too much work."

"Just give me a chance," I say.

He shakes his head, raising his thick, sandy colored eyebrows.

"You think you can miss five weeks of instruction and figure it all out on your own?" he asks.

"I'd like to try," I tell him.

What I know is, he's not that great a teacher. I always had to figure everything out by the book, anyway, or maybe with another student. So I don't think I've missed so much, missing his "instruction."

He's convinced I can't do it, though. Maybe he just doesn't want to be bothered with giving me back assignments. Anyway, he won't sign my form.

At lunch Leticia takes us to Pandora's Box Lunch. It's a little sandwich place, run by a woman who turns out to be Leticia's aunt, Myrna.

"Bacon, avocado, tomato?"

"She always knows what I want," Leticia laughs. "This lady is a mind reader."

"It's not hard. Bacon, avocado, and tomato sandwiches are all this girl ever eats," the aunt says, smiling at me. "Now, what can I get for you?"

"Just iced tea," I say.

When we sit at a table, I try to be kind of sneaky about getting my lunch out of my backpack. It's embarrassing to take lunch into a restaurant, especially if you've just been introduced to the owner. But what can I do? I'm trying to make every penny count until my next check. Rudy doesn't have any money now, either.

"I didn't know I'd be going out to lunch," I explain to Leticia, as I pull an orange and a baggy with a peanut butter and jelly sandwich from my pack.

"I take my lunch sometimes, too," Leticia says.

"Let me guess. Bacon, avocado and tomato?"

"Hey. You're a mind reader, too."

We laugh about that, and about other stuff, getting silly over nothing. Laughing that way, freely, reminds me of Daphne, and all of a sudden I miss her. I wish I knew how to get in touch with her.

"So . . . where'd you go all of a sudden?"

"I sort of ran away, but everything's good now, so I don't even want to talk about what made me run away. You know?"

Leticia nods her head. "But it was because of Rudy, wasn't it?"

"Now you're the mind reader," I tell her, only this time we don't laugh.

"It doesn't take a mind reader," she says. "You were so squirmy in class when those people were talking about abuse, I thought you'd crawl out of your skin. And then, there were all those bruises."

"Was it that obvious?" I say.

"Probably not. I just noticed, that's all."

"It's so embarrassing," I say, looking away from Leticia.

"*You* shouldn't be embarrassed. *You're* not the one beating up on people."

"Well, that's all over now. I just want to forget about it."

Leticia says, "I understand."

I'm not sure if she does or not, but it's nice of her to try.

"I did meet a really nice person at the shelter," I tell her. I dig around in my backpack and find the envelope with the pictures Rudy didn't want to look at.

"Here," I say, passing them across the table. "You'd like her. She's fun, and easy to talk to, like you."

Leticia picks up the stack of pictures.

"She's really pretty, isn't she?" Leticia says, pointing at Daphne.

"Yeah. And a nice person, too."

"What's her name?"

"Daphne."

"And the kid?"

"Kevin. He's three."

"And this is your little girl? Cheyenne?"

"Yeah. She's two."

Leticia comments on each picture, noticing details, asking questions. I wish Rudy had been that interested.

Myrna comes over and refills our drinks.

"How's your mom today?" Myrna asks Leticia.

"She's better. It's just a cold."

"Stop back after school and get some of my good bean soup to take to her. That'll get her on her feet."

They both laugh, then Myrna goes to wait on someone else.

We talk a little longer. Leticia fills me in on the high points of what's been going on in Peer Counseling. She tells me a little about her ex-boyfriend, speaking of him in a way that makes me think she'd like to get back with him.

I complain to her about Mr. Horton refusing to sign my form.

"He's a throwback to the thirties," she says. "He thinks flexibility is a nasty word."

"To him it's the 'f' word," I say.

That gets us laughing again, and then it's time to go back to school.

Ms. Sullivan shakes her head.

"You've got to finish these five credits of math or you won't be able to graduate."

"But I'll have over two hundred and twenty credits without it," I say.

"I know, but it's not only the numbers. You need thirty credits of math, and without this course you'll only have twenty-five. Summer school — you can graduate after summer school, or you can do what I suggested earlier and finish up at Sojourner or through Independent Studies."

"But I want to graduate from Hamilton, in June."

"Well, you've missed too much math. Actually, I'm surprised

your other teachers are letting you back in. I know Ms. Lee has high standards."

"I kept my grades up at Desert Dunes," I remind her.

"Well . . . but the math doesn't transfer."

"Couldn't I finish math in a different class — not Mr. Horton's?"

Ms. Sullivan shakes her head. "I'm afraid your choices are clear. Graduate from Hamilton after you finish math in summer school, or finish at Sojourner or Independent Studies and participate in the alternative school's graduation."

I sit there, going over all three choices in my mind. I don't like any of them. Why does Mr. Horton have to be such a butt-head about this?

"Think about it and let me know what your decision is in the morning. I get in around seven. Okay?"

"Okay," I say.

When I go to get Cheyenne, I tell Bergie of my math troubles.

"Well, Sojourner's got a good program," she says.

"But I want to graduate on stage, from Hamilton. I've been here over two years, the longest of any school, ever. And I want my diploma to say Hamilton High School," I say, looking down, trying to hide my tears.

Bergie puts an arm around me but says nothing.

We've had a late dinner, and Cheyenne took a long time going to sleep tonight. It's after eleven by the time I finish cleaning up the kitchen. Rudy's drinking beer and watching some old movie that's got him laughing like crazy. When the phone rings, he answers, then hands it to me.

"Melissa? It's me, Ms. Bergstrom."

"Oh, hi," I say, wondering why she's calling. Rudy is watching me, not laughing anymore.

"Listen, I know it's late, but I had an idea that might work for your math credits."

"Really?" I say.

"Yes. I just talked with a friend who teaches math at Sojourner, and he may be able to help you work something out. I wanted to talk with you before you go back to see Ms. Sullivan in the morning."

"Cool!"

"I'm not positive, but I think it might work. Come see me first thing in the morning."

"Thank you!" I say, and hang up.

"Bergie can help me work things out for graduation," I say to Rudy. "I'm so happy!"

Rudy looks at me, stone-faced.

"What is it? What's the matter?"

"You're a lot happier about fuckin' graduation than you are about me! That's what's the fuckin' matter! And I don't want no teachers buttin' their noses in around here. She had no right to call here!"

Rudy stands, knocking over the TV tray in front of him. He throws his beer can into the kitchen, aiming, I guess, for the trash. The can hits the wall and spews what's left of the beer onto the floor. I sit still as a sphinx. Rudy slams out the back door. I hear him start his car and peel out the driveway.

I feel myself sinking, trying to erase these last minutes, to pretend this is another happy day.

11

It is after three in the morning when I hear Rudy's car in the driveway. It takes him a while to get the door unlocked. I hope that doesn't mean he's drunk. I pretend to be asleep, at the outside edge of my side of the bed. He falls onto his side of the bed, still in his clothes, shoes and all. In an instant he's snoring. He always snores when he's had too much to drink.

Rudy's still asleep when Cheyenne and I leave the house and get into the Teen Moms van early in the morning.

After I get Cheyenne settled in the play yard with Ethan and Brittany, I go inside to talk to Bergie.

"You'd have to do a whole semester's work in Mr. Raley's class," she tells me. "Everyone there works at their own individual pace, so it's possible. The thing is, your pace would have to be triple-time."

"I'll work hard — it'll be worth it."

"It's computer math — completely different from Mr.

Horton's class," Bergie says.

"So I'd go to Sojourner for one class each day, and do the rest at Hamilton? And graduate on stage?"

She nods. "I talked with Ms. Sullivan. She wasn't bubbling over with enthusiasm, but she'll give you a waiver to take an off-campus class."

"I'm *so* relieved," I tell her.

"I'm not sure you should be so relieved just yet. It's going to be hard to do a whole semester's worth of work in just five weeks. Plus you'll have to get yourself over there every day."

"Maybe Rudy'll have time to take me, since he's not working yet."

As soon as I say Rudy's name, I get a funny feeling, but I don't want to think about it.

"Well, for today I'll take you to Sojourner to get you started. I've got to take some materials over there, anyway."

That's better for now, I think. By tomorrow, Rudy won't be mad anymore — probably.

"You can get the Teen Moms van to bring you here after school, just like you've been doing at Hamilton. But you're on your own for the in-between transportation."

By the time I'm finished with my last class, I've got a load of back assignments. A whole book to read for contemporary literature, along with the paper that's due in a week. And that's just make-up. There's also a short story assignment and a test next week. I'm way behind in biology, too. If I hadn't gone to the shelter I wouldn't have to deal with making up all this work. Oh, well.

Sojourner High looks a lot like Desert Dunes, except it has trees and grass instead of sand. But there are only those metal kind of buildings and it's about one-tenth the size of Hamilton High School. Probably not even that much.

After we drop off a pile of workbooks at the office, Bergie walks with me into a room that's filled with computers. A short, dark haired guy smiles and waves at Bergie.

"Be with you in a minute," he says, then turns his attention back to a computer screen and the student sitting in front of it.

"Go back to the edit file and see if you can figure out how to fix it," he says to the student.

He watches a moment, then comes over to where we're standing.

"You must be Melissa," he says, extending his hand to me.

I always feel weird, shaking hands. Like maybe I don't do it right or something. Anyway, we shake hands and he shows me to a computer.

"See you tomorrow," Bergie says.

Mr. Raley hands me a workbook and explains about the class.

"If you do all of the assignments in this book, to at least an eighty percent competency level, you'll have your five credits, plus you'll get a certificate of competency that's helpful in job interviews — if that's anything you're thinking about."

I do think about jobs. I know I'd like a career, not just low paying part-time work, like Irma, or racetrack work, like with my mom. I'd like to go to college, but right now that seems about as likely as my earlier ambition to walk on the moon.

I open the book. Database. Field definitions. Browsing layouts. Calculation formulas. Maybe this wasn't such a good idea after all.

"My student aide will help you get started. I'll check back with you at the end of the period," Mr. Raley says.

He motions to a guy who is sitting at a back table doing paper work.

"This is Jerry. Jerry, this is Melissa. Help her get set up, will you?"

"Sure," Jerry says. He smiles, showing braces on his teeth. It's a nice smile, even with braces. He's really skinny, with thick glasses and plastered down hair. His clothes look like they're from a Penney's discount catalog. But why should I even notice that? I'm a Kmart shopper myself. I sure don't have anything to be getting all snobbish about.

"Have you ever used a computer before?" Jerry asks.

"In ninth grade, for about a week. We did Print Shop stuff."

He laughs. "Didn't everyone? My ninth grade class made enough banners to decimate a forest."

I laugh, too. Decimate. I like the word.

"First thing, how to turn on a computer."

By the end of the period I've worked through the first three assignments. Of course Jerry was sitting beside me, telling me what to do, and there are fifty assignments in the book.

Mr. Raley comes to my desk and asks, "How'd it go?"

"She's a natural," Jerry says.

A natural idiot, I think, but I'll let them figure that out for themselves.

"What do you think?" Mr. Raley says, tapping the book.

"I want to do it," I tell him, not at all sure that I can.

"Okay. I'll sign you up officially."

Together we fill out some forms and then I go to the gate to wait for the Teen Moms van.

Yvonne, another teen mom who I sort of know, is waiting, too.

"I thought you went to Hamilton," she says.

"I do, but I'm taking a math class here."

"Computer math?"

"Yeah. I need the credits to graduate," I tell her.

"Good luck," she says. "I couldn't get through it — had to go back to an easier class."

"Well, it *does* seem hard."

"I think you've got to be some kind of brain, like that Jerry guy who practically lives with computers," she says.

"How's your baby?" I ask, wanting to change the subject.

"Oh, God," she sighs. "He's got another ear infection and he kept me up all night. He's sick all the time."

I nod in sympathy. I'm so lucky Cheyenne is healthy and happy. A lot of the babies at the Infant Center are sick more than they're well. With all I've got on me — if Cheyenne were sick all the time . . . God. Suddenly the thought that I could be pregnant fills me with fear. Even though we only did it once . . . well . . . one night, and day . . . I think back, count up. It was only for a period of about a day and a half before we started using condoms.

My hands are all sweaty and my heart is beating fast. I don't think I could take it, another baby, what with Rudy being the way he is, and Irma still all mad. I try to block the thought. Maybe it's okay. Probably it's okay.

"Melissa!"

I look up to see Yvonne leaning from the van window, looking in my direction. Grabbing my backpack, I step inside the van.

"I've been calling you," Yvonne says, with an expression somewhere between confusion and irritation.

"Sorry. I was thinking."

When I get back to the Infant Center, Rudy is there waiting.

"Where you been?"

"Sojourner High, getting set up for math."

"Let's go," he says, his face set in that stony look I had hoped never to see again.

I gather up Cheyenne's things and call her from the play-house.

"How'd it go?" Bergie asks.

"Good. It's hard, but I'm determined to do it," I tell her.

She laughs. "I bet you were a 'baby-help' baby when you were little, just like Cheyenne is now."

I laugh with her, but inside I feel sad. My mother never told me anything about what kind of baby I was, or what cute things I did. All I know about my early life has to come from my memory, and it's hard to remember back to being two years old.

Rudy is watching from the doorway, still stony-faced.

"Come on, Chey-Chey," I say. "Let's go."

She struts out of the playhouse singing the ABC song. She is so smart, and cute, my worries dissolve when I see my girl.

Rudy says nothing on the way home. I don't care. I don't much want to talk to him, either. Once inside, I get to work washing dishes, putting in a load of clothes, straightening and dusting the living room. Rudy sits in front of the TV watching "Geraldo." Cheyenne stands on a chair and measures soap into a little cup, then dumps it in the machine. She looks for a long time at the empty cup, its sides dusty with soap powder.

"No drink!" she says, shaking her head vigorously.

"Noooo," I say, very serious. "That would be bad for you."

"Bad!" she says, throwing the cup into the still open washing machine.

I retrieve the cup and put it back on top of the detergent box. Taking Cheyenne from the chair, I give her a big kiss and set her in front of the cupboard where we keep pots and pans. I hand her a spoon to stir with. She can play there while I get dinner started.

"I don't want you going to that school!" Rudy yells from the living room.

I look inside the refrigerator and see that Irma's bought stuff for salad, and some hamburger.

"You hear me, damnit?" Rudy yells.

I turn to face him. "I hear you, Rudy. Probably the neighbors even hear you."

"I don't want you goin' to that low life school," he says, his words now quiet and mean-sounding.

"It's the only way I can get the math credit I need," I tell him.

"Fuck the math credit! You're not goin' to that school!"

"You can't tell me what to do, Rudy Whitman! I'm taking math at Sojourner and I'm going to graduate!"

Rudy stands abruptly and kicks the wrought iron magazine stand across the room. Magazines go flying and the rack hits the wall with a bang.

Cheyenne stops stirring her empty pan and looks first at him, then at me, then stands beside me, hugging my leg. I reach into the cupboard and take out a bag of rice. Rudy comes up behind me, gripping my arm.

"Don't get me mad, Melissa," he says, tightening his grip. "I love you is all, and I don't want you hangin' out with gang bangers and punks."

"Let go. You're hurting my arm!"

"Don't hurt Mommy," Cheyenne cries, pushing at Rudy.

He pushes her away and squeezes my arm even tighter.

Cheyenne cries louder, watching Rudy.

"You don't love me," I tell him. "You don't care about me at all. All you care about is pushing me around. And babies. You like to push babies around, too."

As much as I don't want to cry, I can't stop the tears.

The headlights from Irma's car flash across the window as she turns into the driveway. Rudy gives my arm a final, painful squeeze, and shoves me against the counter. Then he goes back to the living room, puts the magazine rack in place, and is stretched out in front of the TV by the time Irma walks through the door.

I pick Cheyenne up and hold her close, trying to comfort her. I rub my arm, feeling a knot already forming. How could I have expected things would be different? I'm such a fool.

Irma puts her purse and a sack of groceries on the table, then reaches out for Cheyenne.

"How's Gramma's baby?" she asks, reaching for her.

Cheyenne, still crying, hides her face in my shoulder.

"What's wrong?" Irma says. "Doesn't Gramma's baby feel good?"

"Daddy-Mama-Owie," Cheyenne says, muttering the words together, keeping her head down.

I know Cheyenne is telling Irma about what just happened, and how Rudy hurt my arm. But Irma doesn't get it. Maybe Irma doesn't want to get it because she doesn't want to face how messed up her son is — or how messed up her own life was with a husband who beat up on her.

Irma stands watching us, looking from Rudy, sulking in the living room, to me and Cheyenne, both trying to stop crying. For an instant I think Irma's hard shell might crack. She might see that I'm not the main problem here. Our eyes meet, briefly, and she looks away.

I wipe Cheyenne's face with a damp paper towel.

"Say hi to Gramma," I tell her, forcing a smile.

"Hi, Gramma," she says, almost in a whisper.

"Sweet baby," Irma says, kissing Cheyenne's neck. "Come to Gramma now?"

Cheyenne leans toward Irma. "That's better now," Irma coos.

Her tone turns to all business when she asks me, "Did you find the hamburger?"

"Yes, I was just getting ready to start dinner when you drove in," I tell her. "Hamburger Helper and rice and salad?"

"Let's just do hamburgers," she says. "I bought buns."

I nod, knowing that when Irma says "let's" do something she means for me to do it. I put the rice back in the cupboard, get the hamburger from the refrigerator, and start making big, thick patties, the way Rudy likes them.

Irma, still carrying Cheyenne, goes to the living room and

sinks into her recliner with a sigh.

Maybe if I think about something besides Rudy I can stop crying. I try to think of something happy and end up remembering when Daphne and I took the kids to the park, and how we laughed and took pictures and played with the kids. It was a "freedom time," is what Daphne said. The memory dries my tears.

"Oooh, I'm tired," I hear Irma say to Rudy. "My boss says for you to come see him around two-thirty in the afternoon if you're interested in the job."

"That's not a good time," Rudy says. "That's when I have to get Melissa at school."

"Since when?" Irma says. "Isn't the van running tomorrow?"

I slice tomatoes and onions, listening.

"I don't want her riding the van anymore," Rudy says.

I pull leaves from the head of lettuce and wash them, keeping the water running low, so I can hear.

"I'm about at the end of my rope with all this," Irma says, waving her arm in a gesture that takes in the whole house.

I put the lettuce, tomatoes and onion on a big plate and place it in the middle of the kitchen table.

"I can't support you, and a baby, and Melissa, and your *car*, and pay the rent, all on my own, while you sit here day after day watching TV."

Whenever Irma gets mad, she says how she supports us all, as if I weren't paying more than half her rent with my checks.

"Four mouths to feed," she says. "It counts up."

I put catsup, mustard, mayonnaise and pickle relish on the table.

"By the time I was your age, Rudy Whitman, I was supporting my mother, not the other way around."

"Okay!" Rudy says. "Just shut up about it!"

Now I hear nothing but the steady drone of the TV while I finish setting the table and fry the hamburger patties. Cheyenne comes back into the kitchen and stirs her pot some more. I turn the patties, pour iced tea into glasses, and empty a bag full of potato chips into a bowl.

"Dinner's ready," I call to the silent TV watchers.

"Time to wash hands," I say to Cheyenne, picking her up.

She reaches her hands under the faucet. I turn on the water and soap up her hands. She rubs and rubs, front and back and between her fingers, like I've taught her to do. Then she rinses all the soap off and keeps rinsing, laughing at the feel of the water. I dry her hands and set her in the high chair. Irma and Rudy are already at the table, chomping into their hamburgers. I sit in the chair closest to Cheyenne and cut food into little bites for her.

"It's a good job, Rudy. If you work hard and are dependable, they'll move you right up. The night manager's about your age and he makes real good money."

Rudy nods, chewing a mouthful of food.

"And it's clean, and steady. Not like construction where you're out of work any time it rains."

"More!" Cheyenne says, pointing to the potato chips.

"Finish your meat," I tell her, "then you can have more chips."

"You've got to keep a lid on that temper of yours, though," Irma says.

Rudy picks up his plate and carries it back to the living room where a news program still drones on.

Irma finishes her dinner, not talking. Leaving her dirty plate behind her, she kisses Cheyenne on the cheek and goes to her bedroom. I sit feeding Cheyenne, picking at my own food, not hungry. I wonder what people talk about, on Sesame Street, or in Mr. Rogers' neighborhood, when they sit down to dinner.

12

It is starting to get light out when Rudy moves close to me in bed and reaches for my hand. I lie quiet, hoping Rudy will drift back to sleep.

"I love you, Missy," he says.

I sigh, wanting to believe him, not knowing what to say.

"I get scared you'll leave me again," he says.

In the dark I feel the knotty bruise on my upper arm.

"I don't want to leave you," I say. "I want us to get along — all happy days."

"We will. I promise," he says, pushing my nightgown up.

"Maybe, if we went to one of those support groups . . . "

"We don't need that support group stuff," he says, rolling over on top of me. "I know what we need."

I feel him pushing at me. I open my legs for him, but it's as if I'm somewhere else, floating over the bed instead of in it. When I first came back from the shelter, sex felt like love. I was wild for Rudy, wanting him all the time. Now the love part seems missing. I just want him to hurry up and get it over with.

When Rudy drops me and Cheyenne off at the Infant Center he gives me a quick kiss, then leans down to kiss Cheyenne.

"Mama-Daddy-Owie," she says, frowning and backing away.

He looks at her, frustrated, then tells her, "Whatever."

He turns back to me. "I've got to go see that guy at my mom's work — get her off my back — but I want you to come straight home after Hamilton."

"But Rudy . . . "

"No! You go over to that low life Sojourner school and you'll be sorry! I guarantee it."

He looks me in the eye for what seems like a long time, then peels out down the street. Bergie jumps at the squeal of tires. When she sees it's Rudy acting up, she looks toward me and shakes her head. I turn away. What can I say?

"I forgot a couple of books that I planned to take to Sojourner yesterday. Do you need a ride today?" Bergie asks.

"Sure," I say. "I haven't got a bus schedule yet."

"And Rudy's not picking you up?"

"He's got a job interview today."

"Well, that's something," Bergie says.

For a while it seems as if things are going to be okay. Rudy started out part-time at Kinko's, but two people quit the same week he was hired, so he got moved to a full-time schedule right away. Sometimes he even gets overtime. Rudy's happier when he's busy and has money coming in, and when Rudy's happy, I'm happy, too.

Mostly he works a swing shift, starting at three in the afternoon and getting off anywhere between eleven at night and one in the morning. So we don't see much of each other these days. Cheyenne and I are usually asleep when Rudy gets home from work. At least Cheyenne's asleep. I'm either asleep or pretending. And then Rudy's still asleep when I leave for school. Or maybe he's pretending, too.

I think that night Rudy yelled at me and hurt my arm really affected Cheyenne. If Rudy's sitting in a chair, or stretched out on the floor, she walks way around him, out of his reach. I'd kind of like to talk to Bergie about it, see what she thinks it means, but then I know one question will lead to another, and I'm not sure I want that. Maybe I'm as bad as Irma, not wanting to look at the total picture.

The main contact I have with Rudy these days is the telephone. Always he calls right after I get home from school. It's not like he has much to say — more like he's checking up on me. Then, later, there's a silent phone call. I'm pretty sure it's Rudy. Every night sometime between nine and ten, the phone rings. By that time, Irma's in her bedroom with the door closed, so I always answer the phone. I say hello a couple of times, and when I get no answer I hang up. Every night that Rudy's working this happens. It never happens on his days off, when he's home.

Anyway, Rudy hasn't said a word about me staying away from Sojourner since he started working. I guess he's been too busy. I'm glad. I don't want to fight with him about it, but I'm for sure going to finish the math class and graduate on time, on stage.

At first, computer math seemed way too hard, like I'd never understand it, but now it's all beginning to make sense. What I really like about it is how the computer gives the same response each time I do a particular thing. Like if I go to the "catalog" file, and open "data entry," the same thing will come up on my screen, every time. The computer is *not* moody. I like that.

When Cheyenne and I get home from school Thursday afternoon, I see that the answer machine is blinking. There's a message for Irma from her sister, and a message from my mom. I can hardly believe my ears. I tried to call her after I left the shelter, just to let her know where I was, but I couldn't reach her. So then, I called Sean's mom, who said she'd get the message to Mom. But I never heard back.

On the recording, Mom leaves a new number and says she's going to be in Los Angeles for a while, and she'd like to see me and Cheyenne. I call back.

"June Fisher here. Leave a message."

That's my mom all right — no wasted words.

"This is Melissa. I'll call back later," I say, and hang up, disappointed.

It's been nearly a year since I've seen my mom. Not that we're mad or anything, we just never seem to get around to it. I guess that shouldn't bother me, but it does sometimes. Leticia's always got some story about her mom bringing home something new for her to wear, or giving her some wise advice. I think I'd like that.

Now that Rudy's not usually home for dinner, Irma and I don't sit down together. That's fine. It's easier because I don't have to fix a regular dinner, and there's not so much clean-up to do. Honestly though, sometimes I miss the shelter. There was always someone to talk to there, and in group meetings we talked about things that really mattered to us, and there was always something going on. Maybe it's just me. Maybe I'll always feel lonely wherever I go.

I bring Cheyenne's ABC train puzzle into the living room and help her with it and try to read at the same time. *I Know Why the Caged Bird Sings* is the title of the book. It's a true story, about the early life of a famous black woman. It's hard to understand how people can be so awful to each other — like white people not letting black people drink from the same fountains, or go to the same schools — or, on the other hand, those black guys that beat a white truck driver almost to death, just because he was white. I hope all that race hate stuff is over by the time Cheyenne gets to school. Well, it won't be, I know. But I hope it is, anyway.

"Look Chey-Chey, you've got ABCDEF, now what comes next?"

She picks up a Y and tries to make it fit.

"No, try singing the song. Remember?"

Cheyenne sings the ABC song while I point to the letters that are already in place.

"A, B, C, D, E, F, G . . . "

"Yea! G's next," I cheer her on. "Can you find a G?"

She looks at the big plastic letters strewn all around her. I pick up a J, an L, and a G and place them in front of her.

"It's one of these. Which one is the G?"

"Right there!" she says, poking the G with her index finger. "See 'em?"

"Yea! You're so smart!"

We both laugh and she works to make the G fit. I read a paragraph, and then see that she's trying to put a Y next to the G.

"No, look, Cheyenne. What comes next?"

I start singing the song and she joins in. And we go through the routine all over again. It's not the easiest way to read a book, one paragraph between puzzle letters, but I don't want to be like some of those moms who dump their babies in front of any old TV program just to get them out of their hair. "Sesame Street," or "Mr. Rogers," or "Barney," that's okay. I know Cheyenne learned the alphabet song on "Sesame Street," and she knows how to count to ten, too. That's from "Sesame Street." But I don't plop her in front of junk TV.

It is after nine when Cheyenne is settled down, bathed and asleep. I pick up my book again. I'm only on page thirty-six, 210 pages to go and there's a test on it Friday. I can't tell yet, but

I think *I Know Why the Caged Bird Sings* may end up being one of my book friends. I think it has more to say to me than *Go Ask Alice* did.

Reading about how a "spirit-filled" woman knocked the preacher's false teeth out in the middle of a sermon has me laughing out loud. I'm thinking how Maya Angelou sure knows how to tell a funny story, when the phone rings. It's probably another one of those mystery calls, but I answer anyway.

"Hello?"

"Melissa?"

"Mom?"

"What have you been doing?"

"Do you want a whole year's worth, or just today?" I say. I don't mean for it to come out sarcastic, but it does.

"In general," she says.

"Well, taking care of Cheyenne, going to school, keeping up with the laundry and housework, mainly that. What about you?"

"I'm settling down."

"What do you mean?" I ask.

"I'm tired of the circuit. I got on at Convention Center Services in L.A. You know, where Teresa works now. I want to stay in one place for a while."

"You're not working the track anymore?"

"Nope."

I can hardly believe it. That's all I've ever known my mom to do, go from racetrack to racetrack.

"I'd like for you and the baby to come over to my place. Teresa and I got a place together. It's not much, but we're close to a park, so it would be fun for the baby . . . You know, that business of moving every meet, four or five times a year — it gets a little old after twenty years or so."

"It was old to me by the time I got to first grade," I tell her.

"Yeah, well. Water under the bridge," she says. "So, do you want to come on Saturday?"

"Sure," I say.

She gives me her address and I tell her we'll try to get there around noon. Really, I want to talk to Teresa as much as I want to see Mom. I always wonder about Sean, and I'm sorry we've lost track of one another. It's so easy to lose track. I have no idea where I could reach Daphne anymore. She's just gone.

I'll have to call MTA and see what the best way is to get to my mom's new place. Maybe Cheyenne and I can make an adventure of it — riding the big bus, or maybe even the Metrolink. I've never been on that before, and Cheyenne loves seeing the little trains zip along the railway near the freeway.

"Hey! Who were you talking to tonight!"

At first I think I'm dreaming. Then I feel a strong poke at my back.

"I asked you a question!"

I turn to see Rudy standing over me, looking down with the look I don't like to see on his face. I rub my eyes and glance at the iridescent numbers on the clock. Two-thirty-seven. I get a whiff of stale beer fumes.

"Who were you talking to on the phone tonight, damnit!"

"Shhh, Rudy, you'll wake Cheyenne up," I plead.

"Answer me!" he yells.

"I was talking to my mother," I tell him.

He lets out a snort. "You expect me to believe that?"

Cheyenne stirs. I get out of bed and walk to the living room, Rudy following close behind. If a fight's coming, Cheyenne doesn't need to see it. In the living room I turn to face Rudy.

"It's the truth. My mom called. Listen, her message is still on the machine."

I press the play button but before he can hear even the first word he punches erase.

"That don't mean nothin'! You probably had someone from

that loser school call and leave a message. Anyone could pretend to be your mom. You think I'm stupid?"

He shoves me and I trip backward, landing on the couch.

"Huh? You think I'm stupid?"

"Yes!" I scream, standing to face him. "Yes! You're stupid! I was talking to my mom! That's all!"

"SHUT UP!" he yells over me, but I keep yelling back. I am so angry, I don't care what he does to me.

"Why would I lie to you, Rudy? I've been right here, taking care of our baby, and cleaning your mom's house, and fixing your lunch for tomorrow and doing my homework! And if you think I've been doing anything else, then you're *STUPID!*"

He smacks me in the face and I smack him right back. Irma rushes from her bedroom and pushes between us. Rudy shoves her aside.

"Stop, Rudy. I won't have this in my house anymore!"

Rudy shoves her down on the couch and starts pacing, back and forth across the room, again and again, like a caged tiger. He keeps looking at me, even when he turns and changes direction.

"I know what you've been doing, bitch!" he says in that quiet, measured voice that is more frightening than yelling and screaming can ever be.

Irma gets up from the couch and puts her hand on Rudy's shoulder. He pushes her away, not even pausing in his tracks.

I stand, watching, following his pacing, not blinking away from his hate-filled eyes.

"That Mr. Raley from low-life high school was in getting stuff copied today. Your *name* was on the paper — some kind of sheet spread or something."

"Spread sheet," I tell him, my voice as hateful as his. "He wants to use my spread sheet as an example."

"Yeah . . . I asked him, 'Who's this?' all innocent, and he says one of my star students!'"

"So?"

He stops and faces me, inches away. "So, I told you to stay away from that place! That's *SO!*"

His fists are clenched and his face is so stony it looks like it would chip away if you took a sculptor's hammer and chisel to it. I picture my hands, holding the tools, chip, chip, chipping away at Rudy's stone face. Chipping away lines of hatred, chipping away his nose, and his chin, and the vision gets me laughing, and I can't stop laughing and laughing in his stone face.

He stands silent, stunned, and I keep laughing. I don't mean to. I can't help it.

"Stop!" he yells, shoving me backward onto the couch.

The laughter keeps coming until I am weak with it.

"STOP!" he demands. He kicks me in the shin, hard. Pain shoots through me. Sharp. I catch my breath and then laugh harder, sharp and fast, like the pain.

"You slut! Boning that Raley guy to be his *star*! Whore!" Rudy yells, reaching back for the magazine rack, swinging it overhead and down at me. I jump aside, just in time. It breaks the wooden trim on the side of the couch clean in half, like a well-placed karate chop. Rudy looks at the bent frame of the rack, confused, as if it had bent itself and somehow managed to jump into his hand.

I laugh so hard I wet my pants, and that's funnier still. I can't help it. I look up at Rudy. Stony face, chip, chip, chip, I think, and laugh harder still. He stands, puzzled now. He doesn't know his face is chipped away. He looks down at me.

"Stop," he pleads, "please."

Irma comes to the couch with a cold cloth and wipes my face with it.

"Stop it, Melissa," she says, almost gently.

Rudy sits down on the footstool across from me, his head in his hands. I turn my back to them and stifle my laughter in the cushion of the couch. I don't know when my laughter turns to weeping, or when they leave the room, or when someone covers me with a light blanket.

Sometime before dawn I limp into the bathroom and check my skinned, bruised shin. I wash it gently and spray it with Bactine. The colors, red, pink, brown, purple, remind me of one of Daphne's pictures, except her array of colors was all over her body, not just her shin. Just the shin isn't so bad.

I limp lightly into the bedroom and change nightgowns. Cheyenne is sound asleep, gripping Mary. I stand looking at her for a moment, filled with love. I don't look in Rudy's direction.

Next I clean the couch cushion with warm sudsy water. Running my hand over the break in the couch's wood trim, I know the force of that blow could have killed me.

For a moment I picture it, the wrought iron rack coming down full force against my head, the split skull, the instant darkness. Then the thought of not being around to love and protect Cheyenne hits me hard in the pit of my stomach. What would become of her without me? I sit on the couch, thankful to be alive, and to know that I'm the first one Cheyenne will see in the morning, and the last at night. Then, I toss my still damp nightgown into the washer and start a load of clothes, put a towel over the damp spot on the couch, and lie there until the day's first light shows at the edge of the living room drapes. My shin throbs.

13

While Cheyenne and I are waiting in the driveway for the Teen Moms van to pick us up, Irma shuffles out in her bathrobe, her hair sticking up all over and her eyes barely open. It's about three hours before Irma ever gets up, except on those rare times when she has to cover an early shift for someone at work.

"You better not have any crazy ideas in your head about taking that baby away again," she says.

"The only idea I have is to finish my credits so I can graduate," I tell her, shifting the still sleepy Cheyenne in my arms.

"No court'd give you custody, you know — hysterical laughing jags, crying jags, peeing your pants, no means of support."

Irma pauses, then changes her tone.

"I'll talk to Rudy," she says. "I know he's not perfect. He shouldn't be acting that way."

"If that magazine rack had hit me . . . "

"I know. I know. He shouldn't drink at all 'cause it just gets him going. I'm gonna tell him to stop."

"Like you have so much influence over him," I say, thinking

how he shoved her around last night.

"You didn't have to make things worse with your back talk! I've warned you about that mouth of yours."

For a moment, I see that same hard look on her face that Rudy gets when he's being the Rudy I don't like.

"I'm telling you, Melissa, don't do anything crazy. I won't be so nice this time. If you're not here when I get home from work today, I'll have the cops on your tail in no time. You pull another stunt like before and you'll lose this baby forever."

Cheyenne stirs and smiles. "Gramma," she says.

Irma softens. "Good morning, Sweetheart. Gramma loves you."

"The van," I say, standing with Cheyenne, grabbing our backpacks and limping to the open door and up the steps. Cheyenne waves out the window until we're at the end of the block, and Irma stands waving back.

In English my mind keeps wandering. I run a finger over my pants leg, where my bruised and pounding shin is hidden from sight. Over and over my thoughts get caught in a replay of last night. The magazine rack smashing against the arm of the couch. Rudy's stony face. I should have gone to the halfway house, stuck it out, like Daphne did. But now . . . could Irma really take Cheyenne away from me? Just thinking about it gets my heart pounding fast. I try taking deep cleansing breaths, like I learned to do in the shelter. It helps a little, but then, when I think again of Irma's threat — it starts all over, pounding heart, sweating palms.

No one loves Cheyenne the way I do. Irma says she loves her, and I guess she does, but I'm the one who feeds her, and bathes her, and takes care of her when she's sick. I'm the one she runs to when she's hurt. God. I can't stand the thought of not being with her. That couldn't happen, could it?

In Peer Counseling we're watching the end of a movie that we started earlier in the week. It's called "Priest" and it's about this gay priest who gets caught with his lover, and then makes the headlines of a tabloid. It's a really good movie, but I can't follow it today. At the end, a teenage girl comes to take communion from the gay priest and he holds onto her, sobbing and sobbing. I don't even know why he's crying, but just seeing it gets me started and I can't stop. Like I couldn't stop laughing last night.

I run from the room, embarrassed, and into the restroom. Leticia follows close behind. I splash cold water on my face, take deep breaths, and gain control.

"This is more than being sad over the movie, isn't it?" she says.

I nod.

"Tell me," she says.

"It's just, things are hard for me sometimes," I say.

She smiles and dangles her keys. "Aunt Myrna's bean soup. That'll help."

I feel too nervous to go to lunch, but I don't know how to get out of it, with Leticia being so nice.

"Okay," I say.

At Pandora's Box Lunch, Leticia orders bean soup for both of us, telling her aunt I need some magic beans.

"That's exactly what I need," I say. "Magic."

Myrna pretends to go faint with surprise over Leticia's order of something other than her usual bacon, avocado, tomato sandwich.

We take our soup and bread and sodas to a small table in the back. It's funny, but Leticia is right about the soup. It helps. After about the third bite, I don't feel quite so stressed. Not that my problems have gone away, but at least my palms aren't all sweaty and my heart's not racing.

"Thanks," I say to Leticia.

"Wanna tell me?" she says.

I take another spoonful of soup, not exactly wanting to talk, and not sure where to start, even if I wanted to.

"Remember back at the beginning of school, that day I was all down about my gramma having to go to a convalescent home?"

I nod.

"And I hadn't told any of my other friends because it seemed too terrible to say out loud. But then, I told you, because you always listen like you really care."

Again I nod, remembering Leticia crying about how her grandmother didn't even know her anymore.

"I felt better after I talked to you. Not that it changed anything, except I didn't feel so closed up inside. You know what I mean?"

"Yeah, I do," I say.

"You know you can trust me not to blab?"

"Oh, yeah, it's not that, I just don't know . . . well . . . "

There's what seems to be a long silence, then I ask Leticia, "Finished with your lunch?"

She looks at me, puzzled.

"Yeah, I'm finished. Why?"

I pull up my pant leg and show her my messed-up shin.

She gasps and leans forward for a closer look.

"Rudy?" she asks.

I nod.

"God, it looks horrible. Have you seen a doctor?"

"It's not broken or anything," I tell her. "I yelled back at him," I explain.

"Nothing deserves that," she says. "Are you going back to the shelter?"

I tell her how Irma threatened to take Cheyenne away from me if I left, and how much I want to graduate on stage, from Hamilton High School, and how confused I am.

"Sometimes I wonder if I'm losing it — like today I couldn't concentrate at all in any of my classes, and last night I was like a crazy woman, laughing and laughing when things were so terribly sad . . . "

"Give yourself a break, girlfriend. You've got a right to be crazy. I'd be crazy just tryin' to take care of a baby and go to school, and I've got a mom who'd be on my side. And I've got aunts and uncles I could go to, too."

Leticia slides a paper napkin across the table to me and I dab at my teary eyes.

"And here you're not only having to do everything on your own, you're takin' all kinds of hits from Rudy and his mom both! You deserve to be crazy!"

Leticia laughs and I do too, only this time it's a real laugh, not like last night.

We sit there, Leticia sopping up the rest of her soup with a piece of bread, me sipping what's left of my Pepsi.

"You're right," I tell her. "It does help to talk."

"Yeah, it does. But you're still in a mess."

I get a familiar feeling and excuse myself to go to the restroom. Inside the stall, I check my underwear. Yes! Something's finally going my way. I get a tampon from the machine and go back in the stall. When I come out, Leticia's waiting for me.

"You okay?"

"Much better," I tell her.

"Listen, if there's ever a way I can help . . . "

"Thanks."

By the time I get to Mr. Raley's class at Sojourner High School, I'm dragging. All I want to do is just curl up somewhere and sleep for days.

There are only seven lessons left in my workbook, and two more weeks of classes. So far, I've not gotten less than ninety percent on any of my work in here. I'm going to make it. I know I am. I make myself find enough energy to get to work.

I turn on the computer, put in my disk and bring up my file. There's the spread sheet that Mr. Raley took to get copied, the one that set Rudy off. Why didn't he just copy it on the machine in the office? Or at the other Kinko's? Then none of that stuff would have happened last night.

I go to the next lesson, another spread sheet task, and for a few precious minutes I'm so involved in what I'm doing that I think of nothing else. Then, as I go to the next step, I realize that what happened last night was going to happen again, no matter what. It could have been anything. Rudy is an abuser, and one way or another he'll find an excuse to abuse me. Usually I just try to forget, but now I try to remember all the excuses he's ever used for hitting me. I open the word processing program and start a list.

REASONS I DESERVE TO BE HIT, ACCORDING TO RUDY:
I talked to a friend.
Dinner was too early.
Dinner was too late.
My lipstick was too red.
I thought he should get his muffler fixed.
I don't like rap music.

I feel someone behind me and turn to see Mr. Raley looking over my shoulder. I quick erase the file and bring the spread sheet lesson back onto the screen. Did he read what I'd written? He's looking at me, eyebrows raised, as if he's got a question on his mind.

"I met your boyfriend yesterday," he says. "Rudy? Is it?"

"Yeah, he told me you'd been in," I say. "Look, is this part right?"

I point to the screen, to something I know is right, but I want to change the subject.

"Perfect," Mr. Raley says, smiling.

"Listen, there's something I want to talk to you about," he says.

My stomach jumps with butterflies. He's seen the list.

"There's a company, Graphic Design Services, out in City of Industry, a bit of a jaunt, I know, but a good company with good benefits . . . "

What's he talking about?

"I work there sometimes, in the summer and occasionally in the evenings if they're desperate for help. Nice people . . . " he says.

What's that got to do with why Rudy hits me?

"I don't even know if you're looking for a job or not, but you'd do well there. They asked for recommendations, and I gave them Jerry's name, and yours."

At first I can't make the transition from thinking he was going to be all upset about the list he'd seen, and he'd know I wasn't really so smart if I let anyone beat up on me, and he'd probably get a social worker to come out and get messed up in my life and . . .

"Of course, if you're not interested . . . "

"No. No, I'm interested," I say. "I just didn't understand at first . . . "

"It'd be in their accounting department — not much money to begin with but plenty of chance for promotion because they're growing so fast . . . "

"When would I start?"

"They want you to come in for an interview next Thursday. I've recommended Jerry, too."

"Oh," I say, disappointed. "Jerry'll for sure get it."

Mr. Raley laughs. "No, it's not like that. There are two openings and I've recommended the two of you."

"Jerry knows a lot more than I do," I tell him.

"Jerry's been in my class a lot longer. But you catch on as

fast as anyone I've ever had in class. You seem to have a gift for learning the ways of computers."

"I like predictable," I tell him.

"Me, too," he says. "I was raised by a mom and dad who were both alcoholics. Boy, do I like predictable."

We exchange a glance, like maybe we understand something below the surface. I still don't know if he saw the list or not.

As soon as Mr. Raley walks away, Jerry pulls a chair up next to mine.

"Did he tell you?" Jerry asks, his braces showing through a wide smile.

"About the job?"

"Yeah. Cool huh? We'll be seeing each other at the water cooler, just like in Dilbert."

I laugh. "What if we mess up on the interview?"

"We won't. We'll practice with Mr. Raley before we go out there. Do you have your resumé done yet?"

"Resumé? I've never had a job in my whole life. What do I have that would go on a resumé?"

"You'd be surprised," Jerry says.

He goes back to the desk where he usually works and prints something out, then brings it back to me. He's listed things like being a counselor at a YMCA Camp, and being an aide for Mr. Raley, and warehouse duties for his mom's Amway business.

"It's only three shelves in our garage, but still, I keep track of stuff, and load and unload materials . . . "

"You drive to school, don't you?" I ask.

He nods his head.

"Maybe you could call yourself a transportation director, too."

"You laugh, but it's all true, and it looks good, too," he says with a smile. "Just wait."

He gets his resumé disk and brings it back to my computer. We copy it, then use it as a guideline for mine. Really, there is more than I thought there would be — as an aide for Bergie I keep her files straight, answer the phone, keep the kids interested in play activities, clean up the sleeping area and keep the toys in order.

"So, you're a file clerk, receptionist, educational play consultant, assistant maintenance engineer, and materials supervisor," Jerry says, entering that information on my resumé form.

Mr. Raley comes back to my computer to see what we're laughing about.

"Very impressive," he says, laughing with us. "You might want to tone it down just a bit, though."

He stands over us, giving us ideas for how to reword things. Then he pulls a chair up and enters a line right after the one I've written listing my experience with computers in his class, "Certificate of Completion, Computer Math, With Special Honors for Excellence."

"Really?" I ask.

"Really. You deserve it," he says, then walks away to help someone else.

"Cool," Jerry says. "I'm getting one of those, too. We're the only ones. I know, because I enter everything in Raley's grade book."

I rush into Bergie's class, full of my news.

"Guess what? I'm getting a special certificate in Mr. Raley's class, and he's got me set up for an interview for a really good computer accounting job."

"Good for you," Bergie says, but she looks more worried than happy.

"Mommy!" Cheyenne says, running to me, arms open.

I scoop her up. "Mommy's going to get a good job, and buy you lots of toys, and new clothes, and new clothes for Mommy, too . . . "

"And Daddy?" Cheyenne asks.

"Maybe," I say.

And then I realize there's a lot I've not thought about in the excitement of good news. I've only thought about how nice it would be to be working, and not on welfare, and I haven't thought at all about who would take care of Cheyenne while I was at work. And I haven't thought about Rudy, or the mess I'm in.

"Cheyenne?" Bergie says, "Would you please take this baby doll to Ethan in the playhouse? I think he was looking for it."

As soon as Cheyenne runs off, Bergie says, "Cheyenne's grandmother was here today."

"Irma?"

"Rudy's mother. Mrs. Whitman."

"Why?"

"She wanted to take Cheyenne — said she had a doctor's appointment."

"No," I say, trying to make sense of it.

"I told her the only person Cheyenne could be released to was you. That's the only name on file."

My heart is racing. Was she trying to take Cheyenne away from me, like she'd threatened?

"I can't take that responsibility, Melissa. If Cheyenne had a doctor's appointment that her grandmother was going to take her to, you should have worked that out with me . . . "

"She didn't have a doctor's appointment," I say, sinking down into one of the toddler-sized chairs, palms sweating, again in a state of fear.

"No doctor's appointment?" Bergie says. "You're sure?"

"No doctor's appointment," I say.

"But she was so insistent. I had to call security before she'd leave. She said she'd be back with a police escort. I told her to come ahead, I know where I stand within the law."

"This morning she told me if I ran away again she'd get the

cops after me and I'd lose Cheyenne forever."

I'm shivering, even though it's about eighty degrees in here.

"Could she do that, Bergie? Could she take Cheyenne?" I ask, through chattering teeth.

"Catch me up with what's been going on since you got back from the shelter," Bergie says, pulling another toddler chair up next to mine.

For the second time today, I spill out my story, only this time I'm more frightened and scared than ever. Cheyenne. I can't lose Cheyenne. What if Bergie had let her go with Irma? What was Irma planning to do?

14

"**Y**ou know more about what's right for you and Cheyenne than anyone else in the world. Don't let Irma or Rudy push you around," Bergie says.

She takes Polaroid pictures of my messed up shin. Some pictures she gives to me and some she keeps for her own confidential file.

She also writes a short report of how I've been injured, and a report about how Irma tried to take Cheyenne without authorization.

"We need to document everything," she says. "Has anyone but Irma ever seen Rudy hit you?"

"No."

"So, if there were ever a court custody case, it would be just your word against theirs."

"Yes, but . . . "

"Keep track of things — dates, what he said, what he did, anything that would indicate he's violent and unstable."

I tell her as much as I can remember about earlier times when Rudy was violent. Mostly I don't remember dates, but a few I do.

"How does Cheyenne respond to her father?" Bergie asks.

"That one time, before we went to the shelter, she got all passive because Rudy'd yelled at her and shoved her down in her crib when she wanted to do her 'Baby help' thing. And now, since she saw him hurt my arm and yell at me, she walks way around him, always staying out of his reach."

Bergie notes that in her file, then turns to me.

"It's not my place to tell you or any other student what to do," she says. "But if you were my daughter instead of my student, I would urge you to take Cheyenne and get far away from Rudy and his mother."

"I don't know what to do," I say. "They won't take me back at the shelter, because I left before I was supposed to."

"There are other shelters," she says.

"But graduation . . . and the job interview . . . "

"I know. Things are complicated. But you need a plan. You're at a crucial time in your life, and if you don't take control, someone else will.

"What's best?" is the question I keep asking myself in the van on the way home. I remember how lonely I got at the shelter, and how Cheyenne was always thinking she saw her daddy, or gramma, and how happy Rudy and I were for a while when I came back. I'm important to Rudy, but in a good way, or a bad way?

At home, I get juice and a piece of toast for Cheyenne and put it on her little plastic table, where she can eat and watch a Barney tape. Then I go sit on the edge of the bathtub and clean my raw and bruised shin. Needles of pain shoot through me every time I dab at it with the washcloth.

Are there enough good times to balance the bad times? It's true, what the booklet on abuse says — even if the violence doesn't happen often, the possibility is always there, a cloud over everything.

"Wow!" Cheyenne says, peering in the doorway and noticing my shin.

"Owie, owie," she says, making a sad face.

"Happen?" she says.

"Mommy fell," I tell her.

"Wow," she says, coming closer.

"Oh, listen, I hear your favorite Barney song!"

She runs back to the living room. I feel sick, not so much from my hurting shin, as from the lie I've just told. Why should I feel like I have to lie to my own daughter?

When I finish in the bathroom I spread my books and notebook on the kitchen table and check my assignment sheet. I'm caught up with everything except a short paper on *I Know Why the Caged Bird Sings*. Then it's only a matter of studying for finals.

I do know how to make a plan. I knew I wanted to graduate from Hamilton, I figured out everything I needed to do to make that happen, I made a schedule for myself, and I followed through.

I wish it were that simple to make a plan for other parts of my life, like Bergie says I need.

When the phone rings I expect another of those silences on the other end, but this time I get a voice.

"Hey, Babes," Rudy says.

"Hi, Rudy," I say, my body tensing at his voice.

"I been thinking, maybe you're right about that support group stuff."

He's practically whispering, so he must be using the pay phone in the employee's lounge.

When I don't say anything, he continues. "That's what you

want, isn't it?"

"I guess," I tell him.

"I know I get carried away. I mean, you should never have yelled at me like that, but I'm sorry I kicked you. And maybe that group stuff would help."

"Maybe," I say. "Let's talk about it when you get home."

"Stay awake for me? I get off at midnight tonight."

"Okay," I say.

"Let me talk to Cheyenne," he says.

I call her to the phone.

"Daddy!" she says, her eyes sparkling.

She listens, then says, "Yuv you, too," and slams down the phone.

Two weeks ago I'd have been totally happy if Rudy'd agreed to attend a support group. But now, with my shin throbbing and bitch, whore, slut still echoing in my head, and with the image of wrought iron smashing into wood, wood that could have been my head, I don't hold much hope for a support group. Still, I know what a sacrifice that is for Rudy, even to consider it.

Cheyenne and I are eating scrambled eggs and applesauce when Irma comes in from work. She starts in on me right away.

"I should be authorized to pick Cheyenne up from the center," she says.

"Why?"

"Why? Because I'm her grandmother, that's why. The *only* grandmother who cares about her."

I give Cheyenne another bite of applesauce.

"Why did you go there today and lie about a doctor's appointment?"

"I just wanted to take her shopping, that's all. She needs some new clothes."

Irma's lying, I know. She's never bought clothes for Cheyenne yet, why would she start now?

"You sign a paper, or whatever it is you have to do, so I can pick her up if I want to."

"Hey, Cheyenne, more egg?"

Cheyenne clamps her mouth closed.

"More applesauce?"

She shakes her head.

Irma moves closer. "Don't you ignore me, Melissa! I want authorization, you hear me?"

I look up at her. "I hear you."

"I'll pick her up and take her shopping, tomorrow, before I go to work."

"You want to take her shopping, the three of us can go on Saturday," I say.

"Are you telling me you won't fix it so I can get her from the center?"

I wipe Cheyenne's face and hands and take her out of the high chair, then stand face to face with Irma.

"You threaten me, that I'll lose my baby forever, and then you expect me to fix it for you so you can take her whenever you want? I'm not *that* stupid."

"I don't know what's got into you lately," Irma says. "When you first came here you were so nice and easy to get along with, and now you act like you think you're better than anyone else."

I carry our dishes to the sink, wipe the table, and fill the sink with hot, sudsy water. I sink my hands into the water, nearly to my elbow. It feels good — soothing.

"How's your leg?" Irma says, quieter.

"It's sore, but it'll heal."

"I wish Rudy didn't get like that. He's just like his father."

"I don't think that should be an excuse," I tell her.

"Yeah, well, you make things worse sometimes, too. You should just humor him when he gets like that."

"It's not my fault," I say, wondering how many more times

we'll have the same argument.

Irma sighs, watching me wash dishes.

"I'll tell you this. I'm going to get authorization over Cheyenne. You can make it easy or you can make it hard, but I've got rights, too."

I may not have my plan all figured out, but one thing I know is, Irma getting authorization over Cheyenne is *not* part of any plan I'll come up with.

Irma picks Cheyenne up and carries her into the living room. She turns on the news, full blast, and then sits with Cheyenne in the recliner.

"Want ice cream, Chey-Chey?" I call to her. I've got to be really loud to make myself heard over the TV. I think Cheyenne would hear "ice cream" whispered in the middle of a rock concert, though.

She comes running. "Ice cream!" she says.

I don't give her much sweet stuff, but it's a good excuse to get her away from the TV without fighting Irma. She knows I don't like Cheyenne watching the news with her. It's way too violent.

I put Cheyenne back in her high chair and scoop vanilla ice cream into her plastic "Lion King" bowl.

Irma gets up and goes to her room, not bothering to turn off the TV. She slams the door behind her. I guess she's mad that Cheyenne's back in the kitchen with me.

I'm drying the last dish when I hear the announcer say something about "nineteen-year-old Daphne Coulter . . . "

I rush to the TV in time to see a flash of one of the pictures she carried around, of the back side of her bruised body, and then, and then the Sunday church picture of her and her family.

I sit down, weak. What is it?

" . . . suspected history of abuse, though neighbors say Dean Coulter was always nice, ready to help anyone out."

And then it switches to a business report. God! What is it? I switch channels, again and again, West Africa, basketball, the President. What is it? Maybe if I call the TV station . . . Frantically, I punch 411 and ask for the number for Channel Four.

"What network might that be?" the operator asks.

"Network?"

"ABC, CBS, NBC?"

"I don't know!"

"I'm sorry . . . "

I get a glimpse of the Sunday picture again and drop the phone.

"Found dead early this morning in her neatly maintained house in Fontana. Her son, age three, was sitting beside her, trying to feed her a banana."

It is as if there is no air in the room. I can't breathe. My mind is stuck. Daphne dead, Daphne dead, Daphne dead, is all that's in it.

"Mommy! Mommy! Mommy!" slowly breaks through. At first I think it must be Kevin, trying to wake his mother, but it is Cheyenne, standing precariously on her high chair tray. I rush to her and swoop her into my arms. I take her to the bathroom where I strip her and run a tub of warm water. I lift her into the bathtub.

"Baby help!" she says.

"I forgot," I tell her.

I hold her hand while she climbs out of the tub, then climbs back in by herself. She gets her yellow ducky and swishes it around in the water, making quacking noises. I think of the time she and Kevin played with the duckies, and how Daphne and I sat in the bathroom with them and laughed our heads off. I turn my face from Cheyenne and lean against the cabinet. Sobs erupt from a place so deep inside me I didn't even know it was there. Shaking, shivering — life is so hard. Poor Daphne. Poor Kevin. Why did she go back? Kevin with his banana. I cry so hard I throw up.

"Mommy sick," Cheyenne says, making her sad face.

I swear, if it weren't for Cheyenne I'd just give up, here and now. But there she is, skin all wrinkly from too much time in the tub.

"Come on, Chey-Chey," I say, holding out my hand.

"Baby help!" she reminds me.

"I know," I tell her.

I wrap her in a towel, wash my face, brush my teeth, and take her into the bedroom to get her ready for bed. It is eight-thirty. Three-and-a-half hours before Rudy gets off work. Irma won't come out of her bedroom until morning, unless there's an earthquake. The TV is still blaring away.

"Can you turn the TV off for Mommy?" I ask Cheyenne.

She runs from the room, still naked. The noise stops, and then she's back. I diaper her, then hand her her best pajamas. She struggles, trying to get her feet in after she's already put her arms in.

"Feet first, silly," I say.

"Silly," she echoes.

I help her get her arms out of her pajamas so she can start over again. I put an extra pair of pajamas, four T-shirts, jeans, shorts, a dress, and as many diapers as will fit into her backpack. From the kitchen I get juice, crackers, and some jars of baby food. I hardly ever give her baby food anymore, but sometimes it comes in handy.

"Going?" she says.

"Maybe after a while," I tell her. "Here, climb into your crib with Baby Mary."

"Story," she says, frowning.

"I don't have time now, Chey-Chey. How about if I just sing to you while I get some things together?"

"Bushel," she says.

I open my drawer and reach in the back, under a sweatshirt,

and get out the papers — birth certificates, social security cards, medical records, my journal from the shelter.

"I love you, a bushel and a peck, a bushel and a peck and a hug around the neck," I sing to her while I stuff things into my backpack. I don't even know where I learned the song. It's just something I've always known.

My books and notebook take up so much room I hardly have room for clothes. What else? Bactine and Tylenol. My mom's address and phone number in my pocket. Leticia's address and phone number.

A backpack over each shoulder and Cheyenne in my arms, I turn off the bedroom light and walk on tiptoe out the back door. Slowly, avoiding well-lit streets and stepping into the shadows whenever I hear a car coming, we make our way toward Leticia's.

"Going?" Cheyenne asks from time to time.

"To visit a friend," I tell her.

I keep thinking I'll stop at a pay phone and call Leticia, see if she can come get us. But the only places I know where there are phone booths are on bright corners or in stores. I don't want to take a chance of anyone seeing us.

It is after eleven when we finally come to Leticia's house. I check the address to be sure it's the right place. There are no lights on. I tap lightly on the door, then wait. I hope her mom won't be mad. When no one comes I ring the doorbell.

"Who is it?" a voice calls from behind the closed door. I think it's Leticia. I hope.

"Melissa," I say.

Leticia opens the door a crack.

"I need help," I tell her. "Just for tonight."

I'll say this much for Leticia, she barely blinks before she opens the door wide.

"Come in," she says in a whisper.

She ushers us down the hallway and into her bedroom. It's filled with track trophies and class pictures, even a picture of her T-ball team from when she was five years old. There's a prom picture and a big family picture. I recognize her Aunt Myrna.

"See 'em?" Cheyenne says, pointing to picture after picture.

"I saw the news tonight," Leticia says. Then, tentatively, "Did you?"

I nod.

"That was your friend, wasn't it?"

"Daphne," I tell her.

"I was sure of it. I picked up the phone to call you, but then, I know how Rudy is about you getting phone calls, and I didn't want to cause any trouble, but God . . . "

"I just feel so awful," I tell her. "And so sad for Kevin."

"Kevin?" Cheyenne repeats.

"Yeah. Kevin," I say, trying to sound cheerful. "Your friend. Remember?"

"Miss 'em," Cheyenne says.

"Yeah, I guess there's always someone to miss, huh?" I say, thinking how she'll have to start missing Rudy and Irma again.

Leticia holds her arms out to Cheyenne, but she turns her face away and clings to me. Some people get offended when Cheyenne does that but Leticia just laughs.

"I don't want to put you out," I tell her. "If I could just stay here until morning . . . "

"I've already figured it out," Leticia says. "You and the baby can sleep here, and I'll take the extra bed in my mom's room."

"What'll your mom say?"

"She won't even know the difference. She sleeps like the dead," Leticia says.

We both get real quiet. Tears well up in my eyes.

"Oh, I'm sorry. What a stupid thing for me to say."

"No. It's just . . . I'm so sad."

We sit on the bed, not talking. Cheyenne starts snoring her soft little snore.

"Why don't you two go to bed?" Leticia says. "Unless you want something to eat first?"

"No, thanks," I say.

"See you in the morning, then . . . Here, you can sleep in this if you want to."

She takes an old track shirt from her top drawer and tosses it to me, then leaves, closing the door softly behind her.

I lay Cheyenne on the side of the bed next to the wall and crawl in beside her. I fish around in my notebook for the pamphlet we got in Peer Counseling before I ever even thought about going to the shelter. I read it again.

> *YOU HAVE THE RIGHT TO: Be treated with respect; be heard; say no; come and go as you please; have a support system; have friends and be social; have privacy and space of your own; maintain a separate identity.*

I'm not sure how to make those rights come true. But I'm going to try. I turn out the light. There is a heaviness within me, in my heart and in the pit of my stomach. My eyelids feel so heavy I doubt I could open them. I don't even try. The sleep of the dead, I think. I wonder what that means — what it means for Daphne. I hope it's one of those freedom times that she likes so much, and that came her way so seldom.

15

At first, when I wake in the still dark morning, I don't know where I am, or why there is such an ache within me. Then I remember Daphne and Kevin, and I feel the dull pain of my raw shin. I move closer to Cheyenne, to feel her regular, untroubled breathing.

Before anyone else is stirring, I take my journal from my backpack and start writing. The first thing that comes to my head, and onto the paper, is how much I've missed writing in my journal. But even when no one was home, it didn't feel safe enough, or private enough, to write any of my real feelings while I was at Rudy's.

Now I write a stream of bottled up thoughts and feelings, and then I try to focus on a plan. First I've got to find a place to stay, and I know it can't be near Hamilton Heights, and Rudy.

I'm dressed and getting Cheyenne ready for the day when there's a light tap on the door.

"Melissa?"

I open the door.

"I need to get my clothes," Leticia says, yawning.

She slides open the mirrored closet door and fumbles around for something to wear. I notice she has a lot of clothes. Right now, I'm wearing one of the three outfits that make up my whole wardrobe.

"Hey, Cheyenne," Leticia says, flashing a big smile.

Cheyenne smiles back.

"That's Leticia," I tell her.

"Lisha," she says.

Leticia laughs and hands Cheyenne a stuffed elephant from the dresser.

"Mine!" Cheyenne says.

"Well, it's on loan to you for now," Leticia says.

"Mine!" Cheyenne insists.

Leticia laughs, then turns back to me.

"Mom says I can take the car today. What time do you need to take Cheyenne to the Infant Center?"

"Seven-thirty, but I can't take her there today."

Leticia looks puzzled, then says, "Oh. Because of Rudy's mom?"

"Daddy!" Cheyenne says when she hears Rudy's name. "Work?"

"Yes, Daddy's at work," I tell her.

"I guess she understands everything we say, huh?" Leticia says.

"Seems to . . . I just know they'll come looking for us," I say, avoiding using any names.

"I talked to my mom. She said you could stay here for a while if you need to."

"That's so nice . . . "

"We could be like sisters — I've always wanted a sister," Leticia says, looking at our contrasting side-by-side images in the closet door mirror and laughing.

"I've got to get farther away," I say, liking the idea of sisters, knowing it's sort of a joke.

"No way would anyone believe we're sisters, anyway," Leticia says. "Not only are you Miss White Girl to my glowing ebony, you're about half my size."

Leticia stands tall, displaying at least six inches more height than I can come up with, even on tiptoes. Cheyenne stands beside me, jumping to show how big *she* is.

"Scrambled eggs for everybody?" Leticia's brother yells down the hall.

"Yes!" Leticia yells. "But not all dried up like you cooked them yesterday!"

"Maybe you just ought to get your butt out here and show me how," he yells back.

"Arthur!"

"Sorry, Mom . . . " then to Leticia he yells, "Maybe you just ought to get your *be*hind out here and show me how."

Leticia laughs and I hear her mom laughing, too, from some other part of the house.

I repack our stuff, checking to be sure we have enough diapers for the day.

"Where will you go if you don't stay here?"

"My mom's got a place in Echo Park. I'm pretty sure we can stay there for a while."

"I thought your mom wasn't even around?"

"Well, in and out. Mostly out, but she's not mean or anything. I think she'll let me stay."

"Maybe you should call her first," Leticia says, looking worried.

"No. I think it would be easier for her to say no on the phone. I'll just go over there. I've already checked bus schedules. The 341 goes near where she lives."

"I'll take you," Leticia says.

"You'll be late for school."

"I haven't been late all year long, I guess this one day won't hurt. You don't want to be sitting at a bus stop up on Main, where everybody'll see you, including you know who and his mother."

"Well . . . "

"No problem," Leticia says.

We all sit at the table together, Leticia's mom, her brother, Leticia, me and Cheyenne. Mrs. DeLoach puts two thick phone books on top of a chair and sets Cheyenne on top.

"Now you can reach," she says.

Arthur, who's on the football team and looks it, plays peek-a-boo with Cheyenne until she forgets all about breakfast.

"Let her eat, Arthur," Mrs. DeLoach says.

"I'm going to take Melissa and Cheyenne to her mom's place this morning," Leticia says.

"Where's that, Baby?"

"Echo Park," Leticia answers.

"What about school?" Mrs. DeLoach says.

"It's okay this once," Leticia says.

Mrs. DeLoach looks from Leticia to me, and then watches Cheyenne for a bit.

"Well, okay," she says. "But be careful. That's kind of a rough neighborhood over there."

"I could go with them, for protection," Arthur says, flexing his muscles in a body builder pose.

"You're going to school, young man," Mrs. DeLoach says.

There's some talk about who's doing what today, a family barbecue coming up Sunday, lots of normal, TV sitcom stuff. Everyone rinses their own dishes and puts them in the dishwasher. Leticia washes the skillet and I wipe the table. Maybe this is how it is on Sesame Street, or in Mr. Rogers' neighborhood.

Before we leave, I call Bergie to say I won't be there today.

"Your boyfriend and his mother showed up early, demanding to know where you and Cheyenne were."

"What did you say?"

"I told them the truth, that I had no idea where you were. But they were very rude, yelling about how you'd run away. They barged into the crib room looking for Cheyenne — woke Ethan from a sound sleep.

"I left last night. I should never have gone back," I say.

"I can't have people carrying on like that in here. My first concern is for the safety of these children. I've filed a police report and I'm getting a restraining order on both of them. If either of them shows up around here, or any school property in the whole district, they'll be arrested."

"I don't want to miss school."

"No, but you're probably smart to stay away at least for a few days. A restraining order is good in theory, but it's not always effective in practice."

"I'm so close to graduation, and the job interview, but . . . "

"Call me back around four today, when I'll have more time to talk. Maybe I can help you work some things out."

"Thanks," I say, hoping Bergie doesn't hear the catch in my throat.

I hope there'll be a time in my life when I don't feel like crying so much. When people do something nice for me, like Leticia telling me I could stay here, or Bergie wanting to help, I get weepy. And then there's that other stuff I feel like crying about, Daphne, and Kevin with his banana, and the way Rudy's treated me, and Irma, too. And not really having a home, not living a Sesame Street life, where everyone respects one another.

We check the map and figure out how to get to my mom's. It looks pretty simple, the 10 Freeway to the Hollywood Freeway, then off at Glendale Boulevard to my mom's street. Except we miss the turnoff to the Hollywood Freeway, and when we try to get back to it we get hopelessly lost.

"Look, there's City Hall," I say, pointing to a building in the next block.

"We shouldn't be anywhere near City Hall," Leticia says. "I hate this place."

"We should be going the opposite way."

She frowns and changes lanes abruptly, causing the guy behind us to slam on his brakes and lean on his horn.

"Oh, God, I hope he's not one of those freeway shooters," Leticia groans.

It is nearly eleven by the time we find my mom's address, but there is no place to park.

"Just pull over by that red curb and I'll get out."

"What if she's not there? Or what if it's not the right place?"

"If you can wait here just a minute, I'll go check and come back and wave to you."

"Okay. If a cop comes, I'll circle the block and come back."

I unstrap Cheyenne and get our stuff, then run inside the apartment building and find number twelve.

"Who's there?" my mom yells through the closed door.

"It's me, Melissa," I yell back.

She opens the door and stands aside.

"You're a little early, aren't you? Like three days?"

"I'll explain in a minute. I've got to go tell my friend you're here, so she can leave."

I dump the backpacks on the floor, just inside the door, and hurry with Cheyenne back outside.

"It's okay," I wave to Leticia.

She gets out of the car to wave back.

"Call me," she says, then she's back in the car and gone.

I'm all nervous. My mom didn't light up with joy when she saw me at her door.

"We're going to see Gramma," I tell Cheyenne.

The door is left partly open for us and we go inside. Mom is sitting on the couch with a cup of coffee, checking out the racing section of the newspaper.

"Look, here's your Gramma, Cheyenne," I say.

Cheyenne hides her face in my shoulder.

"I wouldn't have recognized her, she's so big," Mom says, standing to get a better look.

"Want Gramma," Cheyenne says.

"Look, Baby. Here's Gramma," I tell her, turning so she'll face my mother.

"Not Gramma!" she screams. "Want Gramma!"

Mom sits back down on the couch.

Of all the times for Cheyenne to be unfriendly, this is the worst.

"Listen, Cheyenne, this is Gramma, too. You have a Gramma Irma, and a Gramma June. This is your Gramma June."

"Want Gramma Irma!" Cheyenne screams.

"She's tired, and hungry. Mind if I give her a bite to eat and try to put her down for a nap?"

"I haven't been grocery shopping."

"I've brought some lunch stuff for her, just if there's a quiet place I can lay down with her . . . "

"Use my bed," she says, pointing in the direction of a bedroom.

After I give Cheyenne some vegetables and rice, and a glass of juice, I take her into Mom's bedroom and lie down with her. There's not much in the way of furnishings or decorations — a bed and small dresser, no lamps, just a light overhead, no bedside tables. It has the minimum necessities, as suits a person who never stays long in one place.

On the dresser is a picture of me at around four, on top of a horse in the winner's circle. My mom and the horse's trainer are standing together. The trainer is holding the horse's reins. We are all smiling broadly, as if it's a happy time. I know about pictures though, how they can lie, like the Sunday church picture of Daphne and her family. I wonder what the *truth* is of this picture. For as long as I can remember, that picture has been on Mom's dresser, from track to track, the only picture ever on display anywhere she briefly calls home. I've always been curious about it, but every time I'd ask, her answer was the same — "That's water under the bridge."

I wonder if it's there because of the trainer? Or the horse? Or me? Maybe it's there because of my mom. I think she looks pretty in that picture, prettier than I can remember ever seeing her in person.

When I'm sure Cheyenne is asleep, I tiptoe out to the living room where my mom is still on the couch, head leaning back, eyes closed. I sit in the chair opposite her.

"Mom?"

She half-opens her eyes.

"I'm sorry the baby doesn't know me. My fault," she says.

"Well, maybe she can get to know you now."

"I called because I know it's been too long. I see how things are with Sean and Teresa, how they enjoy each other, and I know I've missed some things."

Her eyes are open now, watching me. It feels as if we're two boxers, circling, jabbing, trying to figure out what's next.

"How is Sean?" I ask.

"Good. He's doing good," she says. "Getting his diploma through CCC and starting college in September."

"Where is he?"

"Some national park. Sequoia, maybe," she says.

She seems tired, beaten down, and I wonder if she has a hangover.

"Mom, Cheyenne and I need a place to stay, just for a little while."

"It's not a very good time for me, Melissa."

"Just a month, or even a couple of weeks . . . "

I notice a picture in the paper, half hidden by the Sports section. I pick it up, my heart pounding. It is a picture of Kevin, still holding a grubby banana, looking like a deer caught in the headlights of an oncoming car. Next to his picture is the hospital picture of Daphne's brutalized back, and next to that is the Sunday church-day family picture. Daphne smiles at me, as if she were alive. Cleansing breaths, one, two, three . . . The paper rattles in my shaking hands and I sob with the silent question of Why? Why? Why?

Mom sits watching, puzzled.

"My friend. My good friend," I tell her, pointing to Daphne's picture. I take the other pictures from my backpack, the ones from the freedom time at the park, and show them to my mother. She looks carefully, comparing them, reading a bit, shaking her head over the hospital picture.

"My God," she says in a whisper.

I tell her about getting to know Daphne, and the shelter, and the pictures Daphne carried with her — the ones not in the newspaper. I explain, as best I can, why I decided to go to the shelter, and why I decided to leave. Always in the past, when I've tried to talk to my mom, she's had to get up and do something else, or go back to work, or meet the "girls" somewhere. But today she sits very still, listening. Finally, I show her the picture Bergie took of my leg yesterday. And then I show her my leg. She shakes her head, but says nothing.

"So Cheyenne and I had to get away, and I didn't know where else to go . . . just for a while," I say, wiping tears. "I'm sorry it's a bad time, but there's a chance I'll be getting a job, so I can help out with expenses, and . . . "

"I didn't mean a bad time with money, though that's never easy. But it's a bad time because I'm sick."

"More than a hangover?"

She laughs a short, sad laugh. "Breast cancer," she says.

I don't know what to say, how to act. It's not like we've ever been close, or all that lovey-dovey mother-daughter stuff, but still . . .

"**I**'ve got a pretty good chance of beating it, but it means heavy-duty chemotherapy, which has a mean nasty side to it."

I look at her carefully now. Her skin looks dry and papery, her eyes dull. Is that the disease, or the treatment, or depression?

"Mom . . . "

"Stay. It'll be crowded but we'll manage."

"It won't be for too long . . . "

"I know I haven't been what you'd call a prize-winning mom. I can do this much, for a while. We'll have to work it out with Teresa, but she's the one's been bugging me to get in touch with you, anyway."

I go into the kitchen and get a drink of water. This has not exactly been what you'd call an overwhelming welcome, or a joyful reunion, but it's a place to stay and I didn't have to beg. I'm relieved about that, even in the midst of wondering what's in store for my mom.

School's on my mind, and the job, and graduation. How can it all work? I go back to the living room where my mom is sitting with her eyes closed again. I take the section of the paper that has Daphne and Kevin's pictures and put it up on a high shelf, where Cheyenne won't see it. I want her memory of Daphne and Kevin to stay pure. It is too soon for her to have to carry such a heaviness in her innocent heart.

CHAPTER

16

While Mom and Cheyenne sleep, I make a list of things to do. I want that job. Just the thought of getting off welfare is a dream come true. Ever since I was four months pregnant with Cheyenne, I've been getting welfare checks. When I hear people complain about high taxes and welfare moms, it's like they're calling me a thief. And whenever I have to go to the office, or talk with my social worker, I feel like I'm nothing — less than nothing. So a chance for a real job is something I don't want to miss. I need to call Mr. Raley and find out more about the interview. Which is tomorrow. What can I wear?

My list:

1. *Call Mr. Raley about job interview (plus figure out clothes and babysitter).*

2. *Call Bergie about school in general.*

3. *Call each of my teachers about how to turn in work and get full credit for the semester.*

4. *Change address at welfare office (again! yuck!)*

5. Try somehow to get clothes and toys from Irma's house?
6. Call other shelters in case this doesn't work out with Mom.

I've got a lot to figure out, and my leg hurts, and I think about Daphne a lot, and I'm pretty sure my mom doesn't want us here. Also, I can't help noticing that my list is probably very different than any list Leticia would be making right now. Like, it doesn't include picking up a cap and gown, or getting tickets to the Senior Breakfast, or buying a new outfit for Grad Nite at Disneyland, or checking to be sure I've got the right dorm assignment for college in September, or any of the things senior girls without babies are doing at this time of the year. Not to complain, but I can't help noticing.

I go into the bedroom and lie down next to Cheyenne. She's been asleep a long time. I rub her back, gently, and she stirs, then opens her eyes.

"I need company," I tell her.

She jumps up and starts bouncing on the bed.

"Five monkeys jumpin' on the bed," she says, bouncing and bouncing.

This is not what I had in mind. I grab her and put her back down on the bed, leaning over her, trapping her. I skip to the punch line.

"No more monkeys jumpin' on the bed," I say, wagging my finger at her and laughing.

"Yes!"

She jumps up again and continues. "One fell off and hit her head."

I grab her again. "No more monkeys jumpin' on the bed."

We laugh and laugh until we finally get through all five monkeys. I change her and take her out in the living room. Mom half-opens her eyes, and half-smiles. Cheyenne looks at her.

"Gramma June?" she asks.

Mom's smile broadens. She searches in her pockets and pulls out a set of keys, dangling them toward Cheyenne.

"Want to play with Gramma June's keys?" she asks, still smiling.

I put Cheyenne on the floor and watch as she takes slow steps toward my mother. Without getting any closer than she has to, Cheyenne reaches for the keys and Mom hands them to her.

"You liked to play with keys at that age, too," Mom says.

"Was I like Cheyenne?" I ask, hungry to hear anything about my pre-memory past.

Mom leans her head back again and closes her eyes. My question goes unanswered.

I hope the keys and a few pots and pans will keep Cheyenne occupied while I start on my list of phone calls. There are no toys for her here, of course, and no little yard for her to play outside. I wish I could sneak back to Irma's and get some things. I sure can't afford to buy all new toys and clothes. But I've got to think everything through carefully, not just act on impulse, the way I did when I left the shelter and went back to Rudy.

I call Hamilton High and leave messages for all of my teachers, hoping they'll call me back and we can work things out. I can mail my English paper in, and the last chapter's biology work, but then, there are finals.

When I talk to Bergie she asks if I'm in a safe place, asks how my leg is, asks about Cheyenne. I tell her I'm worried about the interview. Mr. Raley said we should look professional, and all I've got are jeans and Reeboks and three really casual tops.

"Could you borrow something from your mother?"

"It'd be too big . . . and I don't have anyone to babysit while I'm at the interview tomorrow, either. I wish we could put it off a day, so I'd have time to get some things worked out."

"Ummm. I'm afraid that wouldn't make a very good first

impression. They're likely to think that if you can't get to an interview on the appointed day, you'll probably not be very dependable about getting to work."

I talk on, going through my list, telling Bergie how I'm trying to get things worked out.

"How are things with your mother?" she asks.

"She has cancer," I tell her.

There is a long pause. Then she says, "I think you're getting all of your bad luck out of the way during the first nineteen years of your life, and after that, it'll be smooth sailing until you're eighty-nine. Then you'll die a painless, peaceful death and be whisked away to heaven on the wings of snow white angels."

We both laugh. Then I tell her, seriously, "I want to believe that."

"I do, too, Melissa. In the meantime, don't give up. I think you're headed in the right direction."

When I talk to Mr. Raley, he says to meet him at Sojourner High School at four in the afternoon.

"I've arranged for a late interview, so I can take you out there. I missed you in class today, though."

"I'm having problems," I tell him, not knowing where to start. I wish we had one of those phones that transmit a picture. Sometimes it's easier to get started if I just show my raw and bruised leg.

"Ms. Bergstrom called today. She didn't give me a lot of details, but she said it might not be safe for you to come to school for a few days. Plus . . . I noticed the list you had on your computer the other day — you know, reasons for your boyfriend to hit you?"

"Oh."

"So anyway, you've essentially earned the credit you need in my class. It's not a problem if you miss the last week of classes."

"Thanks."

"I hope you can make it for the interview, though. This is a job that could give you some independence."

"I don't have anything to wear that looks professional, and I don't have a babysitter," I tell him.

"How old is your baby?"

"A little over two."

"Well . . . if you can't find anyone to watch her, maybe you could bring her . . . "

"To the interview?"

"Well, the interview part probably won't last more than half an hour or so. She could stay with me for that short time. There's a fountain in a courtyard out there. My kids like to go there and throw leaves and twigs into the fountain. Would she be okay to stay with me?"

"Probably, if there's a fountain. She loves playing around in water."

"Okay. If you're still desperate for a sitter tomorrow, bring her along. I don't know what to tell you about clothes, except that it's important to look businesslike."

When I talk to Ms. Lee, she says I can mail my *I Know Why the Caged Bird Sings* paper to her. She's talked with Ms. Bergstrom, and she understands I have good reason not to be in school right now. Absolutely no way can I miss the final, though. No way. That would mean summer school make up.

"Well, I've got nearly two weeks to figure that part out, right?"

"Yes. And if it would be more convenient for you to take the final on a different day than scheduled, with another class, I'm flexible in that way. But you *must* complete the final and you must complete it in my presence."

"Okay. Thanks. I'll put my paper in the mail to you on

Thursday."

"All right, Melissa," she says. Then, "I hope you get your life straightened out soon."

"Me, too," I tell her, wondering if she's ever had any real problems.

"**M**issy!" Teresa says as she opens the door and sees me sitting on the floor playing with Cheyenne. "Stand up and let me get a good look at you."

She reaches out a hand. I take it and she pulls me up. We stand, eye to eye, almost exactly the same height.

"You're still just as pretty as ever. Isn't she, June?"

Mom opens her eyes and nods, smiling.

Teresa's hair is red, though the last time I saw her it was blonde. She's wearing a black skirt and white blouse, with a plastic name tag that says "Los Angeles Convention Center," and has her name and picture on it. I notice crow's feet at the edge of her eyes, and deeper wrinkles in her forehead, but she looks as energetic and full of life as ever.

"And look at this beautiful little girl. You're beautiful, you know it?" Teresa says, leaning close to Cheyenne.

Cheyenne runs behind my legs, trying to hide. Teresa and Mom both laugh.

"I thought you were coming on Saturday. We were going to fix a big picnic and take you and the baby to the park."

"Well . . . "

"We need to talk about that, Teresa," Mom says, making it sound like there's bad news to be delivered.

"Saturday, or Wednesday, or any day, it's a treat to see you two kids," Teresa says, giving me a quick hug.

She goes to the couch and sits down beside Mom. "What is it we have to talk about?"

"Melissa and the baby need a place to stay for a few weeks. I said we'd work something out, but that I'd have to talk it over with you . . . "

"June, you knew I'd be okay with that, didn't you?"

My mother bursts into tears, something I've never seen her do before. Teresa puts her arms around Mom and comforts her, like you would a child.

"Shhh. You're tired now. Everything will seem easier in the morning . . . Missy, go into the refrigerator and get the plastic bottle that's labeled 'Wednesday #2.' Shake it up real good and pour it into a glass, over ice, and bring it to your mom. Okay?"

In the kitchen I hear them arguing.

"I'm not hungry, Teresa."

"But you need to keep up your strength. You know what the doctor said."

"I don't care. I don't want it."

I bring the concoction back into the living room and hand it to mom.

"Just little sips," Teresa says.

I watch while my mother takes baby sips, and I wonder how bad the cancer is. She really doesn't look any worse than I've seen her look with a bad hangover. But I don't know. I've never been around anyone who has cancer.

It takes Mom about an hour to finish her glass of — whatever it is. Teresa helps her into bed.

"What about Missy and the baby?" Mom says, as they walk into her bedroom.

"We'll figure it all out. Don't worry."

After a few minutes, Teresa comes back out. Cheyenne is fussing, wanting to play with a glass bowl that's sitting on the coffee table. After the third time I tell her no, she hits me.

"No, Cheyenne. No hitting. Do you need time out?" I ask, immediately realizing there's no crib here, no place to make time out work.

"No time out," she says.

"Then no hitting," I say.

Teresa says, "We've got more than an hour of daylight. Do you want to walk to the park and let her run around a bit?"

"That'd be great," I say. "She's used to being outside part of the day, and having plenty of toys to play with."

"The park's a pretty safe place until ten or so, then sometimes the crowd gets rather seedy."

We walk a couple of city blocks, filled mostly with apartment buildings, and then there's this huge park. I was expecting a little playground place, but this place has a big lake, with people fishing all around the edges of it, and giant trees that must have been here forever.

"It's beautiful," I say.

"Yeah, must have been really something in its heyday. But the lake is clean again — for a while it was all scum."

"Water!" Cheyenne says, pointing at the lake. "See 'em?"

She takes off running and I run after her, grabbing her just as she's about to plunge into the lake.

"No, it's too deep," I tell her. "You have to be very careful and not get too close to the lake. Let's stand back here by the tree and watch people fish for a while."

"Okay," she says, running back to the tree.

Teresa and I laugh. "She's precious," Teresa says.

We sit on the grass, under the tree, keeping watch over Cheyenne, who edges closer to a boy who is fishing with a bamboo pole.

"It's safe for Cheyenne down at this end of the lake," Teresa says. "I stay away from the other end. That's where the druggies hang out. Not that they're particularly dangerous, but they leave needles laying around. Late at night, sometimes there's gang stuff, but mostly, in the daylight, it's a pretty nice place to be."

We get caught up, about Sean, and why I had to get away from Hamilton Heights, and what it's like to quit the track after all those years.

I remember how, when I was little, I used to wish Sean and I could trade moms. It was always easy to talk to Teresa, and she seemed to like us. With my mom, it was like we were in the way. But whenever I suggested a trade Sean would laugh and say, "No way, Jose."

I'm too old to be making such wishes now, but it is still a lot easier to talk to Teresa. My mom *did* listen when I told her about Daphne, though. I shouldn't forget that.

Cheyenne comes running back to us, excited.

"Fish! Fish!" she says, pointing to a fish dangling from the boy's bamboo pole.

"Cute," she says, then walks back down close to the boy and watches as he takes the fish off the hook and places it in a bucket. She leans close over the bucket, watching the fish. The boy doesn't seem to mind.

"How bad is my mom's cancer?" I ask Teresa.

"The doctor says she's got about a seventy percent chance of beating it if she sticks with the chemotherapy plus follows the nutritional program."

"How long has she known?"

"The official diagnosis was only three weeks ago, when they did the surgery, but she noticed a lump probably over a month ago. She had her first chemotherapy session four days ago. According to the doctor, by Friday she should be feeling pretty good, and back to normal for the next week. Then she'll have another chemo treatment."

"How long does she have to do that?"

"Depends. Maybe four months, maybe a year."

"Will she lose her hair?"

"Probably."

We sit quietly for a while, watching Cheyenne, who is now busy gathering leaves and trying to throw them back onto the trees.

"I'm glad you're here for a while," Teresa says. "However

this cancer business goes, your mother should get to know you and Cheyenne."

"I guess. I don't think *she's* glad we're here."

"Give her a chance. You may be surprised."

Near sunset, we walk back to the apartment. I give Cheyenne her bath and Teresa makes a bed for herself on the couch.

"I'm not giving up my bed for long," she tells me with a laugh. "But for tonight, I think it's easier. We'll try to come up with a more permanent plan tomorrow."

In the middle of the night, worried about getting everything done that needs to be done, I take my English notebook and *I Know Why the Caged Bird Sings* into the bathroom, which is the only place I can have a light on without disturbing someone who's sleeping. I sit on the closed toilet lid, reading the last pages of my book, thinking about what I'll write for the assigned paper. Rudy crosses my mind, and Irma, and Daphne, and what am I going to wear to the interview tomorrow?

I creep silently into Teresa's room, where Cheyenne is sound asleep. I find my journal and take it back into the bathroom with me. I write, three, four, five pages — my troubles, my hopes, in an outpouring that somehow lightens the heaviness in my heart.

17

I keep looking at my clothes, trying to think what I can do to make jeans and Reeboks look businesslike. Nothing.

Teresa comes out of the bathroom dressed for work.

"Do you have any businesslike clothes I could borrow for a job interview?" I ask Teresa.

She laughs. "My reading glasses are about as businesslike an item as I have."

Mom is sitting at the kitchen table in her bathrobe, sipping another of those drinks.

"What about one of those black convention center skirts?" Mom says. "With the right accessories, that could look sort of businesslike. And your black pumps? You and Missy are about the same size."

Mom's color is better this morning, and she seems more energetic.

"Listen, I've got to get out of here or I'll be late. But you can borrow anything you want from my closet," Teresa says. "And finish that protein drink," she adds, turning to Mom.

"I'd rather have bacon and eggs," Mom says with a laugh.

"Yeah, well, nobody said getting healthy would be fun — don't forget your fish oil capsules," Teresa says, dumping three big, amber colored capsules on the table in front of my mom.

"See you all later," she says with a wave. Then she's out the door.

After breakfast Mom goes rummaging around in Teresa's closet while I get Cheyenne dressed.

"Try this," she says, pointing to one of Teresa's black work skirts and a pink T-shirt she's laid out on the couch.

I put Cheyenne down on the floor by the couch, get "Sesame Street" on TV, then turn my attention to the outfit. To tell the truth, it doesn't look "professional" or "businesslike" to me, but I try it. I guess my expression shows I'm not impressed.

"This is just basic. We'll accessorize," Mom says, blousing up the T-shirt and checking out the skirt.

"The fit's okay, but the skirt's not a good idea. I forgot about your leg."

I look down at my bruised and scabby shin. It's feeling better, but Mom's right, it's nothing I want to display on a job interview.

"Unless . . . " she says, rushing back into Teresa's room and rummaging through a dresser drawer.

"You know, I used to have sort of a flair for putting together an outfit, a long time ago, before I lost interest."

I think of the picture on her dresser, how sharp she looked.

"Here!" she says, pulling out a pair of wadded up black tights and shaking them out. "Not exactly spring colors, but we can make it work."

First I put gauze pads on my leg, so I won't mess up Teresa's tights, then I pull them on and straighten the black skirt. My mom digs up a pink and black scarf.

"To pull the colors together," she explains, as she ties it loosely at my neck.

She brings out a pair of black sandals with a broad heel, and black pumps that are kind of scuffed.

"No prince for you, Cinderella," Mom says, as I try to jam my feet into the pumps.

"I already figured that out."

"Well, I don't think those prince guys are all they're cracked up to be anyway," Mom says. "Try the sandals."

I can get my feet in these, but they're still way too small. My heel hangs out in back and my big toe hangs over the front.

"This is not good," Mom sighs.

"Big Bird!" Cheyenne says with a clap of her hands. "See 'em, Mom?"

"Oh, yeah!" I say. "Big Bird. We love Big Bird, huh Chey-Chey?"

"See 'em, Gramma June?" Cheyenne yells.

Mom laughs. "Yep. I see 'em."

Mom goes into her room and comes out with another pair of black pumps, even more beat up than Teresa's. I slip my feet into them — a pretty good fit. I check myself out in the full length mirror in Teresa's room. I don't know. I guess it's better than jeans and Reeboks, but the vision I get is of a little girl playing dress-up with discarded clothes, rather than the businesslike vision I'm wanting.

When I come out, Mom has the ironing board up and the iron plugged in.

"Give me those things and we'll freshen them up," she says.

"I can do that."

"No, I feel good this morning. I'll be useful while I can."

I watch while she carefully brushes all the lint from the skirt, then turns it inside out and steam irons it. Then she irons the pink T-shirt and finally, the iron turned low, she irons the scarf.

"Here, now try them," she says. "But leave the shoes here."

I check myself out in the mirror again. Better. Mom brings me the pumps, freshly polished and shiny. They're still rundown, but it's not so noticeable. She blouses my T-shirt and reties my scarf.

"It drapes better this way," she says.

She brings blush and lipstick from her room and dabs a little on me. "Just enough for subtle color," she says, then stands back and looks me over, like an artist appraising her work.

"You're a very pretty girl," Mom says, as if she's surprised.

I look away, embarrassed.

"We've got to tame that mop of hair for today, though," she says.

I hear her rummaging around again, this time in her dresser.

"Damn, where is that clamp thing I bought a few months ago, before I knew I'd be losing my hair?" she mutters.

She tosses me a brush. "Work on your hair a while, will you?"

Cheyenne takes the brush from me and stands beside me on the couch, brushing.

"Ouch. Just my hair, not my face," I tell her.

"Sorry," she says, running the brush across my forehead again.

"Oops," she says.

Mom comes out with two old lady comb things and sits on the arm of the couch.

"Here, Cheyenne," she says, reaching for the brush. "Let me work on this a while."

"Mine!" Cheyenne says, grasping the brush with both hands.

Mom goes into the kitchen and comes back with her keys.

"Trade you," she says.

Cheyenne takes the keys and hands over the brush. Mom brushes my hair back on each side and, with the combs, secures it high, away from my face.

"Businesslike," she proclaims. "Now, let's see. Have we

missed anything? Let's take a look at your nails."

She walks me to the bathroom and hands me a fingernail brush and an emery board.

"Hands make an impression," she says. "I'll entertain Cheyenne while you spend a little time on your nails."

When I'm finished, I find Cheyenne and Mom down on the floor, making a city of pots and pans.

"Here's where the giant lives," Mom says, pointing to the upside down pasta pot.

"And Big Bird," Cheyenne says, pointing to another big pan.

"And Little Canary," Mom laughs, putting the small egg poacher next to Big Bird's pan.

I don't remember anything like this. Did she ever do this with me? I stand watching for a few minutes, then pack up our stuff.

In order to reach Sojourner High School by four o'clock, Cheyenne and I start out just before two. It's only about a thirty minute drive, but the bus is a different story. We've got to make two transfers, and I'm not sure how long it will take to make connections.

Between Cheyenne standing on my lap to look out the bus window, and sleeping for a while with her head on my shoulder, and me wrestling the backpack around, I suppose my clothes won't look so fresh by the time we get to the interview.

It is only a little after three when we get off the bus, two blocks from Sojourner High. Cheyenne is asleep. I sling the backpack over my right shoulder and hold her against my left as I walk toward the school. I think about what they might ask during the interview, how I have to remember to speak up and answer questions directly, and not be shy or modest about what I can do.

Then, as I turn the corner to the school, I see it. The back of

Rudy's car, parked right across the street from the gate. I jump to the side, shielded by a wide-trunked tree. What is he doing there? What should I do? He usually has to be at work by three-thirty. Should I wait, hiding? But maybe he has the day off today. Maybe he found out I'd be here today, with Cheyenne. I hold her closer to me. If I could just get inside the school gate . . .

I walk, fast as I can, toward the gate. Rudy's looking in the other direction, toward my old bus stop. Faster. Don't look, I beg.

"Melissa!" It is Jerry, rounding the corner and into the school parking lot.

Rudy jerks his head around and is out of his car in an instant, running toward me. Even from here I can see the stony look on his face. I run, jostling baby and backpack, straight for the gate.

"Mommy!" Cheyenne cries, waking abruptly. I keep running.

Just as I reach the gate, Rudy catches me by the arm, nearly causing me to drop Cheyenne.

"Get in the car!" he says.

"No!"

"Daddy," Cheyenne says.

Rudy reaches for her and I turn away, tightening my hold on her, shielding her.

Jerry comes sauntering up, a smile on his face. "Hey, Melissa . . . "

"Get in the car, bitch!" Rudy yells, pulling harder at me.

"No!" I yell back.

Jerry walks close to Rudy.

"Leave her alone!"

Rudy brushes at him, like he's a fly. He grabs me by both shoulders and starts pushing me toward his car.

"Victor!" Jerry yells for the security guy as he tries to step between us.

I'm holding on to Cheyenne for dear life and I can't shove back at Rudy.

"Get away, asshole," Rudy says, socking Jerry in the mouth and sending him spinning.

Victor comes running. "Tell Jennifer to call the cops and get Mr. Craig out here," he yells to Jerry.

Victor grabs Rudy from behind, and I slip out of his grip.

"Calm down," Victor says to Rudy.

Rudy turns, fist doubled, and smashes Victor in the face. Cheyenne is screaming and I try to run with her but Rudy grabs us again. Victor, nose bleeding, jumps between us and shoves Rudy backward. Suddenly we're surrounded by Mr. Raley and the principal and a bunch of other teachers I don't know. Others grab Rudy and Mr. Raley guides me and Cheyenne away, through the gathered crowd of students, into the principal's office where he sits me down. I am trembly and weak-kneed and Cheyenne is screaming even louder than before.

"Shhh, Baby. Shhh, Chey-Chey. It's okay. Everything's okay," I say, patting her back, kissing her wet cheek.

"Are you okay?" Mr. Raley asks.

"I think so."

In the distance I hear sirens.

"Is Jerry okay?" I ask.

"I'll check on him in a minute."

The sirens are getting closer. I stand at the window and look through half-open blinds to where Victor and Mr. Craig stand, one on each side of Rudy, each holding an arm.

Cheyenne is still sobbing, her face against my shoulder, dampening, I'm sure, Teresa's pink T-shirt.

"Back to class, now," a teacher says, directing students away from the fight scene toward classrooms.

Kids move away, reluctantly.

"Into class, into class," teachers urge their slow-moving students.

Three police cars, one right after the other, skid to a stop in front of the school. Rudy bolts, but three of them are out of the cars, swarming on him. Two crouch beside their car, guns drawn. My heart is pounding.

Mr. Raley stands beside me at the window, watching.

One of the policemen slams Rudy, hard, against a squad car. "Hands behind your head," he yells.

Rudy puts his hands behind his head. They pat him, hard, all over, up and down his legs, his butt, under his arms, every part of the body I've known so well. Then the bigger one grabs Rudy's hands and pulls them behind him while the other one slaps on handcuffs. Rudy winces, but doesn't look up.

Cheyenne turns her head and I sit back down in the chair, before she has a chance to see her dad in handcuffs and to store that scene in her permanent memory bank.

I hear a car pull out and Mr. Raley says to me, "He's gone."

"'Care me," Cheyenne says, catching her breath.

"Yes, that was scary, wasn't it, Chey-chey?"

"Daddy 'care me," Cheyenne says in a whisper, again burying her face in my shoulder.

The lump in my throat grows bigger, and when I glance at Mr. Raley, looking at Cheyenne and shaking his head, I think he may have a lump in his throat, too.

There's a knock on the door and Mr. Raley opens it.

"I'm Sergeant Drake," one of the cops says.

"Norman Raley," Mr. Raley says, extending his hand.

"Is this who he was after?" Sergeant Drake says with a nod in my direction.

"Yes, this is Melissa Fisher and her daughter, Cheyenne."

Sergeant Drake pulls up a chair and sits facing me, and gestures for Mr. Raley to sit down, too.

"Peeceman," Cheyenne says, pointing. "See 'em?"

He smiles at Cheyenne, then looks at me. "Tell me about it," he says, taking a notepad and pen from his pocket. I tell him about today, and he asks about other times when Rudy has been violent. I know Cheyenne is listening. Even though she's only two, she understands a lot that is said. I want to protect her from the worst — like how much her dad hurt me, or the awful pictures of Daphne and Kevin in the newspaper. But hiding things from her seems dishonest, and I always want to be honest with her. It's hard to know what's right.

I answer all of Sergeant Drake's questions, as if from a distance, as if I'm talking about someone else. Cheyenne leans into me, sucking her wrist.

Sergeant Drake writes down my new address and phone number and says they'll be in touch. Rudy's been arrested on three charges of battery. I guess that's because of what he did with me, Jerry, and Victor. And something about being in violation of a restraining order, and trespassing on school property, and I'm not sure what all else. Anyway, there will eventually be a hearing, and I'll have to go to it.

It is four-fifteen when the police are finally finished questioning me and Jerry and all of the adults who saw Rudy pushing me around.

"We can still get to Graphic Design Services if we leave right now," Mr. Raley says. "I hate to have you miss the interview, but, are you up for it?"

"Let me just clean up a bit," I say. I notice when I stand I'm still a bit trembly. Not too bad, though.

"Jerry?"

"Sure," Jerry says, still clutching an ice pack to his mouth.

"Let's see," Mr. Raley says.

Jerry takes the ice pack away, revealing a swollen red upper lip. He turns his lip up and shows a bunch of tiny, bleeding cuts where his lip was slammed into his braces.

"Not too shaky?" Mr. Raley says.

Jerry holds out a trembling hand.

"Steady enough," he laughs.

I go into the restroom and pat my face with a damp towel. My hair is sticking out all over, but I manage to pull it back again with Mom's combs. I smooth my clothes, straighten my scarf, add a little lipstick and go back out where the others are talking.

Cheyenne falls asleep in the van, which is equipped with built-in carseats for the Raley kids, and Mr. Raley gives us a pep talk for the interview while Jerry ties and reties his tie, trying to get it right.

"Remember, you're good. You're both good, and you have a lot to offer an employer. You're smart, you're dependable, you already know a lot about computers, and you know how to get along well with other people."

"Yeah, that's why we're all beat up," Jerry says, smiling a painful smile.

"I'm not talking about getting along with lunatics, I'm talking about getting along with normal people."

The idea that someone like Mr. Raley thinks of Rudy as a lunatic sticks in my brain. I mean, I know Rudy gets crazy sometimes, but a lunatic? And what does it say about me, if I fell in love with a lunatic?

As soon as we turn into the parking lot of Graphic Design Services, there is only one thing on my mind. I want to work here. The fountain in the courtyard, the bright colored flowers bordering walkways, the big pepper tree shading the entrance to the building — please let them like me here, I think, brushing at my skirt and patting my hair.

"I'll just stay here with Cheyenne," Mr. Raley says. "I hope she won't be frightened if she wakes up and finds you gone."

"I don't think she'll wake up, but if she does, do you know the alphabet song?"

Mr. Raley laughs. "As well as my own name."

He gets out of the car and calls Jerry over to him.

"Stand in front of me, with your back to me," he says. Then

he unties Jerry's tie and reties it, so the bottom side is not hanging out past the top side.

"Good," he says. "Go to the receptionist, right inside the door, and tell her you have an appointment with Ms. Fallon."

18

My mom is bustling around the kitchen when I get home, grilling fish and mixing it into a big green salad.

"Just in time for dinner," she says, getting bread from the oven and pouring water for everyone.

There is a tablecloth on the table, and a rose in the center.

"Smell!" Cheyenne insists.

I pick up the vase and hold it out for her. She sticks her nose into the flower.

"Yum," she says.

I stack phone books on a chair and push Cheyenne close to the table.

Teresa comes out of the bathroom, straight from the shower it appears.

"Hey, that works," she says, taking in my "businesslike" outfit.

"Mom figured it out," I say.

Teresa looks at the table, rose and all.

"Good day?" she asks Mom.

"Today I've got my energy back, and appetite. I'll be able to work next week," Mom says.

"At the convention center?" I ask.

"Yeah. They've arranged a schedule for me where I work as I can, between chemo. I have to be able to do a week at a time, not just day by day stuff, but that's better than nothing. I want to stay off disability if I can."

"How long have you been working there?"

"Only about a month before the cancer was diagnosed. Sometimes it seems like human nature is the pits, and then people you hardly know do something really nice — like my bosses at the convention center."

"Bread, pease," Cheyenne says, stretching toward the steaming loaf.

"Right. Let's eat!" Mom waves a piece of bread back and forth, to cool it, then hands it to Cheyenne.

It surprises me that Mom seems so good with Cheyenne when I can't remember her being that way with me. Has she changed? Or was she a better mom than I remember her being?

"All the right stuff," Teresa says, looking over the table.

It turns out that Mom's supposed to have lots of fruits, vegetables, and fish. No meat, no fats. And then she has the special soy protein stuff that she drinks, and the fish oil capsules. It's part of a research project going on at UCLA. Supposedly, they've been having good results with a combination of chemotherapy treatment and this nutritional plan.

"Butter," Cheyenne says, waving her bread around.

Mom and Teresa both laugh. "Sorry," Mom says, "that's not on our grocery list."

"Look, Chey-Chey. Mommy's eating bread without butter."

I take a big bite of butterless sourdough bread.

"Yum," I say.

We all show Cheyenne how we're eating bread without butter. She's not impressed.

"Butter, pease," she says.

She keeps slipping off the phone books. That distracts her from wanting butter, but it also distracts her from eating dinner. I wish I could go back for her high chair, and her carseat, just a few essentials would really help.

"How'd the interview go?" Teresa asks.

"Good, I think. Ms. Fallon said she'd call us in a few days. Her boss is out of town and she's got to get an official okay from him before she can hire us. We had to take a basic math test, which was easy, and then she asked us about what computer programs we'd worked with. We each had a packet of sample work to show her."

"Did she interview you and your friend together?" Mom asks.

"No, but she asked us both the same questions."

"Were you nervous?" Teresa says.

"Yeah, but I'd already had sort of a hard day before I got there."

"Sure. That's an awful bus ride."

"Well, it wasn't that so much . . . I'll tell you later," I say, glancing at Cheyenne. It's enough that she was in the middle of it, and then had to hear about it all over again with Sergeant Drake.

Sometimes it seems like each day is more like two separate days. The one when Cheyenne is awake and almost all I can do is feed her, change her, play with her, watch her, keep her happy. And then there's the quiet day, night really, when she's asleep. That's when I read, do homework, talk on the phone. It's especially like that now that I'm not in school and she's not going to the Infant Center.

The first thing I do after I get Cheyenne settled for the night is call Leticia.

"Hey, Girl. How you doin'?"

"Good," I say. "But I miss school."

"Heard you had a scene over at Sojourner today."

"Who told you?"

"Arthur. He's got friends all over the place. That's his main job, you know, keepin' in touch with his friends and playin' football."

"And Leticia's main job is runnin' off at the mouth," Arthur yells into the phone.

"Get away, Arthur!" she yells back.

I called Leticia *after* Cheyenne went to sleep, so we could have an uninterrupted conversation? I wasn't thinking about Arthur.

"With Rudy in jail, can't you come back to school?"

"They arrested him, but Sergeant Drake said Rudy'd probably be out on bail by tonight."

"I just hate that," Leticia says. "Rudy's bein' a dickhead, so now *you* can't come to school. What kinda fair is that?"

"It's not, but I don't know what else to do. Maybe he learned his lesson today, but maybe it just made him madder and meaner. It's not like he worries about breaking laws — he knew there was a restraining order against him."

"Restraining order?"

"Yeah, Ms. Bergstrom got a restraining order on him when he and Irma went to the center looking for Cheyenne."

"My life is so dull in comparison to yours," Leticia says. "I got no drama."

"Be glad. Your life is like living on Sesame Street," I tell her. "I want a life like Sesame Street."

"My life's not like Sesame Street, except for Arthur, who's exactly like Oscar the Grouch."

"But there's conversation, and people laugh, and treat each other with respect, and you've got aunts and uncles . . . "

"No dad. Does that take me off Sesame Street?"

"If only people with dads got on Sesame Street, they could

only do about one show a month instead of every day," I say.

That gets us talking about dads.

"Do you think there was really a time like old people talk about, when hardly anyone ever got divorced, and people didn't have babies unless they were married, like fifty or a hundred years ago?" I ask.

"Nah. How could that be?" Leticia says.

"Sometimes I worry that it won't be good for Cheyenne, growing up without a dad."

"It'd be worse growing up around Rudy."

"I know, but . . . "

"It's normal. Did you ever know your dad?"

"No."

"Me, neither."

"I missed it though, didn't you?"

"Yeah. But only because of TV. Don't let Cheyenne watch any of those stupid TV programs where there's always a dad hanging around the house — you know, how you're careful about not letting her watch violence? Don't let her watch dads."

That gets us laughing.

Then I feel Teresa standing behind me. "Hey, I don't want to rush anything, but I need the phone pretty soon."

"Oh. Okay. Gotta go. Here's my new phone number. Call me anytime," I say.

It's not until way late at night, after everyone else is asleep and I'm finishing my English paper in the bathroom that I think maybe I got just a glimpse of Sesame Street here, under my own nose, tonight.

We were laughing and talking together at dinner, and then I was able to talk freely on the telephone without being called a slut or getting hit. Even after that awful time with Rudy today, right now, I feel pretty good. I open my journal and write about that.

After I write in my journal, I read the rough draft of my *I Know Why the Caged Bird Sings* paper. I write about how strong Maya Angelou was — even though she was raped by her stepfather, and then felt guilty for it, and she lived in the midst of terrible racism in the south, and her mother and father sent her away when she was only three, even with all these things she grew up to be an important writer and dancer, and even wrote a poem for a presidential inauguration. Those are the main points of what I get from the book.

I say it better in the paper, without having it be one big run-on sentence. The book was inspiring to me, because I see that even though things may be horrible when you're young, it's still possible to make a good life.

It is after three when I fold my paper into the envelope, seal it, address it to Ms. Lee, c/o Hamilton High School, and put two stamps on it. Cheyenne and I will walk to the post office first thing in the morning.

Back in bed, I can't get back to sleep for a while. Even thinking I had a partial Sesame Street evening isn't enough. In my mind, I keep seeing Rudy, his stony face first, but then it softens, his eyes are warm with love. All happy days, he is promising me.

Then I see again the handcuffs locking on his wrists, and I'm sorry for him. I hope they didn't hurt him at the station. I know it happens sometimes, especially with guys who get smart. Rudy might have done that.

But was he worried about hurting me, or Cheyenne, when he was shoving us around? No!! And remember the wrought iron magazine rack whizzing past your head, I tell myself. You could be dead, like Daphne.

Deep cleansing breaths. One . . . two . . . three . . . I envision the fountain, the flowers, the pepper tree out at Graphic Design Services, and Cheyenne at the park trying to throw leaves back up onto the tree — so much is good, so much is awful. Lean toward the good, I tell myself, and finally I sleep.

Friday afternoon Sean arrives at the apartment, sleeping bag slung over his shoulder. Teresa runs to greet him. She kisses him on the cheek and he picks her up and twirls her around, laughing. I can't help comparing their greeting to the way Mom and I greeted each other a few days ago.

"Hey," Sean says, giving me a quick hug.

He leans down next to Cheyenne, who is stacking cans on the floor.

"My name's Sean," he tells her.

She hands him a can of non-fat refried beans.

"Thanks," he says, laughing.

We all sit around the kitchen table, drinking iced tea and talking. At first I feel awkward around Sean. We'd been best friends for so many years, when we were kids, but now we're kind of like two strangers. He looks different. Bigger, more like a man than the boy I used to hang out with, talking all night long. I notice him glancing at me, and wonder if he's feeling awkward, too.

Teresa makes a shopping list for the picnic tomorrow.

"Are your friends coming?" she asks me.

"Leticia for sure, and maybe Jerry."

"Did you talk to Justin?" she asks Sean.

"I just left a message," Sean says.

Teresa makes a grocery list and Sean and I walk to the market. It's the first time I've left Cheyenne with Mom and Teresa, but when I tell her I'll be right back she waves bye-bye without even looking up. I guess she's pretty comfortable with them now.

There's a guy on the corner, asking for money. Sean hands him a quarter and I get a whiff of stale urine as we walk past him.

"The city kind of gives me the creeps, after being in the mountains for so long," Sean says.

"I've never been to Sequoia."

"You should come up sometime. It's beautiful, and quiet, and peaceful."

"What do you do up there?"

"Repair trails, clear fallen trees and branches, maintain campsites, all kinds of stuff. It's hard work — but it's made a man of me," he laughs, pushing up his sleeve and raising a well-developed bicep.

"Really," he says, getting all serious. "It saved my life to go into the corps. I don't know if Mom told you, but I was pretty messed up for a while — drugs, and the petty crime it took to keep using, and then dealing — you know, one backward step after another."

"I didn't know," I said. "I lost . . . Rudy tore up your phone number . . . "

"I knew he was bad news that day I saw him a long time ago . . . tough guy with the girls," Sean says, disgusted. "I wondered why you didn't call me, though."

"It's not that I didn't want to."

"I hear you've been having hard times," Sean says.

We stand outside the market, leaning against a shopping cart rack, talking for a long time. I tell him about the shelter, and Daphne, and how I finally left Rudy for good. He tells me about how he did a lot of things he's ashamed of, and how he was finally arrested, and sent to rehab, and then joined the CCC.

"There are plenty of drugs there, too," he says. "You can find that stuff wherever you go. But I'm through with that now. I'll start school in September, up at College of the Redwoods. I'll major in forestry."

We stand talking so long, it's nearly dark when we get back to the apartment and I'm worried about being away from Cheyenne for such a long time. No one's in the living room or kitchen and I get a sinking feeling that something's wrong. Then I hear laughter coming from the bathroom.

Mom and Teresa are both kneeling by the bathtub, where Cheyenne sits surrounded by floating plastic cups. She fills one, holds it high, and turns it over.

"Waterfall!" the three of them yell, and Cheyenne does it again. Mom and Teresa laugh like it's the funniest thing they've ever seen.

I go back to the kitchen and start making potato salad for tomorrow's picnic. I hope it will be good with non-fat salad dressing instead of mayonnaise. My mom can't eat mayonnaise.

19

Sean and I take Cheyenne to the park a little early, so we'll be sure to get tables. Leticia and Arthur get there shortly after we do.

"I had to bring him, he owns the frisbee," Leticia says in mock apology.

"Yeah, and I had gas money, too," Arthur laughs.

"Aunt Myrna sent this," Leticia says, lifting the cardboard cover from a big sheet cake.

It's got white icing and it's decorated with black graduation caps and tassels. "Congratulations," it says, in big red letters.

"Cool, huh?" Leticia says. "For you and me."

"Sean's graduating, too," I say. "And Jerry."

"Well, then, for you and me and Sean and Jerry."

Arthur reaches a finger toward the icing and Leticia bats it away. "At least let everyone see how pretty it is before you defile it."

"Just a taste for the baby," Arthur says, sneaking past Leticia's guard and scraping a bit of icing from the side.

"Here, Baby," he says, letting Cheyenne lick icing from his finger.

"Yum," Cheyenne says.

Arthur carries Cheyenne over to the swings and Sean, Leticia and I throw the frisbee around for a while. Leticia and Sean are really good at it.

When Jerry arrives I leave the frisbee to the experts.

"Walk with me to check on Cheyenne," I say.

Jerry's lip is still swollen.

"Are you able to eat, or is your mouth too sore?" I ask him.

"It looks worse than it is," he says with an awkward smile.

"I'm sorry," I tell him.

"Not your fault," he says. "Did you hear anything yet?"

"No, did you?"

"No. I guess if we don't hear by Tuesday we should call."

Cheyenne is swinging high, laughing. I introduce Arthur and Jerry, who I think won't have a thing to say to each other. But it turns out that Jerry is a big sports fan, and Arthur's signed up for an advanced computer course. I didn't even realize I'd stereotyped them until I was surprised by their conversation. Oh well, at least I didn't *say* anything embarrassing.

After lunch, Sean and Teresa and Leticia walk Cheyenne close to the lake, so she can watch people fishing. Jerry and Arthur are tossing the frisbee back and forth. Jerry's always seemed to me like a total indoor type, but I see now that he is quick and agile. I sit under a tree, next to Mom, watching the frisbee action, and Cheyenne in the distance.

After a while Mom says, "This cancer stuff really got me thinking."

"You look healthy, Mom," I tell her. It's true, too. I watched her walking up to our table earlier today. Her steps were sure and quick, her brown hair, though thin, was shining in the sunlight. When she called hello to us, her voice was strong. Not like a sick person's.

"I feel great today, but I know there's something inside my body that's trying to take over, trying to kill me."

I pull at the grass by my feet, not knowing what to say.

"At first I thought, okay, life's got me worn out, anyway. Let it go. But then I thought about all I'd missed. And watching Teresa and Sean . . . well . . . I wished I'd been a better mother to you."

I look at her, but she turns her head. I wonder if she's hiding tears.

"Teresa kept urging me to call you, get to know you better, but I thought it was too late. I mean, you're grown up now. I can't possibly make up to you for years of . . . not paying much attention . . . or . . . whatever . . . I'm sorry."

I hear the tears in her voice, and it's hard for me to talk, too, but I say, "If you'd just talk to me about things . . . not turn everything into water under the bridge . . . "

She heaves a big sigh. "What do you want to know?" she says.

Questions whiz through my head, about my father, and my grandparents, and what was I like as a baby, but the question that comes out of my mouth is the most crucial question of all. If it turns out I only get one question, this is it.

"Do you love me?" I ask.

I hold my breath, waiting for her answer.

"My problem, I think, was that I loved you too much."

"It didn't seem like it," I whisper.

"I've thought a lot about that lately, reviewing my life now that I may be nearing the end of it. It seemed to me that everything I loved turned to ashes. My father died when I was four. I have almost no memory of him. My mother, beautiful and full of life, left me in a foster home when I was seven. I never knew why, except maybe I'd been bad, or somehow didn't deserve her love. I ran away from my foster home when I was sixteen and started working at Santa Anita, then from there to Bay Meadows, you know how that goes."

I want to stop her, to ask questions, but she is telling me this as if in a dream, and I'm afraid if I interrupt her, that will be the end of her story. So I listen quietly, hoping no one comes over to where we're sitting.

"I guess you could say I was wild. I'd not had much guidance growing up, just 'do this, do that,' from my foster parents. It's a wild crowd, anyway, that racetrack bunch, drinking, gambling, fighting, living on the edge. I kept up with the best of them, or the worst, however you want to look at it.

And then I got pregnant with you. I don't even know for sure who your father was — could have been one of three, though your hair makes me think it was probably a guy named Wayne."

Wayne who? I want to know. Where is he? I want to know.

"But I loved you from the beginning — quit drinking and smoking as soon as I found out I was pregnant, promised I'd never leave you like my mother left me, no matter what. I think I was a pretty good mother for the first few years, as good as a mom can be who's always on the road and has to work long hours.

But track people, even if they're wild, they're warm hearted. This one trainer took his mother with him wherever he went — Lucky Mama he called her — anyway, until you started school, she took care of you when I was at work.

"We had some good times, though. I didn't have to be at work until noon, so we'd go watch them exercise the horses in the morning. We'd take apples to feed them and you loved to feel their soft noses."

Tears are streaming down my cheeks and I want to ask what happened, what got lost. Teresa walks toward us, then slows, looking at us appraisingly. She goes back to the lake.

"The picture you always used to ask about," she sighs. "That was Benson. I met him at Hollywood Park — really, you met him first. He saw us at the morning workout and came to talk to you, gave you a slice of fig, which you popped into your mouth and then made such a face we laughed 'til we were weak. We loved each other, the three of us, from then on. I'd never known such happiness — didn't even know the possibility of it. He loved me, and he loved you. He was one of those pure-spirited kind of guys that don't hang around racetracks much. He never wanted to hurt anyone, or see anyone hurt, and it was beyond him to tell a lie."

"After Hollywood Park we went together to Bay Meadows. That's where the picture was taken. At the end of that meet we were going to get married. We had the rings and everything. Benson had a job lined up to train horses in Kentucky, to settle into one place. He was going to take us there with him. And then there was the accident, a freak thing with the practice gate and a horse he was training — he was crushed to death in an instant."

She pauses, staring off into space, and I wonder if she'll say anything else.

"Then what?" I urge.

She looks at me as if surprised to see me there, then continues.

"Then . . . then . . . I was lost, shattered. And I think, somehow, in some twisted way of looking at things, I thought it was our happiness that had killed him. Like people don't deserve that much love. And I think, maybe this doesn't make any sense but I've been mulling it over a lot lately, I think I was afraid if I loved you so much, the same thing could happen to you. I was afraid, that's all.

Now there's all this awareness about depression, and grief support groups, and the importance of showing love to children, but then none of that was around. At least not that I ever heard of. Maybe if I'd had some help . . . but I was working it all through, inside, and I guess I got it all messed up."

She is quiet for a while, still looking away.

"Mom," I say, wiping at my tears.

She turns to look at me. She, too, has to wipe away tears.

"Thank you, Mom," I say.

We sit together for a long time. The noises of the park, laughter, leaves rustling in trees, muted traffic noises, wash over me as I replay her story, again and again, in my mind.

At twilight Leticia calls us all over to the table and takes the cover off the cake.

"To us graduates!" She holds the cake cutter high overhead. "We should have a song," she says.

We sing "Happy Graduation to You," to the tune of "Happy Birthday" and get all hysterical at "Happy graduation dear Leticia, Jerry, Melissa, Sean . . . " because everyone sings the names in a different order.

"Bushel and a Peck" Cheyenne demands. Cheyenne and I start out. Leticia knows the song and so does Arthur. I see my mother at the end of the table, her cheeks wet with tears.

"Again," Cheyenne says, and Leticia and Arthur start the song again. It's not all that complicated to pick up on and this time everyone sings, loud and raucous and laughing.

It's hard to explain, but for an instant, when everyone's singing, I feel a glow of us all loving each other a bushel and a peck.

We cut the cake and pass it around. Cheyenne dives in with both hands.

"Little bites, Chey-Chey," I tell her, but it's too late. Her mouth is so full she can barely chew, and that gets us all laughing again.

Later in the evening, after everyone's gone home, we pack up our stuff and head back to the apartment. Sean carries Cheyenne on his shoulders and walks next to Teresa. Mom and I tag along behind.

"Where did Cheyenne learn that song?" Mom asks.

"'Bushel and a Peck'?"

She nods.

"I taught it to her. I don't even know where *I* learned it. It just came out one day, when I was playing with her and she wanted a song."

"We used to sing it all the time, you and me and Benson. I never sang it again, after he died."

"Well, I guess it stuck, anyway," I tell her.

On Monday I hear from Ms. Fallon that I got the job. I'll start in two weeks. There's a one week training program where I'll get paid six dollars an hour, and then I'll get seven dollars an hour after that, when I start my regular job.

I quick add up how much a week that will be — two hundred and forty dollars the first week, then two hundred and eighty. I'm used to getting by on three hundred and fourteen dollars for the whole month.

I call Jerry and get a busy signal. I hang up and decide to make myself wait five minutes before I try again. Just as my five minutes is up and I'm reaching for the phone, it rings.

"Hello," I say.

"Did you get the job?" he says, his voice about an octave higher than usual.

"Yes! Did you?"

"Yes!"

"Can I come see you tonight? We can make plans for work."

"What kind of plans?" I ask.

"I don't know. Just plans," he laughs.

After dinner Jerry comes knocking on the door, two cans of Pepsi in one hand and a little box of apple juice in the other.

"Let's go to that park with the lake," he says.

It seems like I'm spending half my time at the park these days. It's crowded in the apartment though, and there's not much for Cheyenne to do there.

I tell Mom and Teresa we're leaving and grab a diaper for Cheyenne, just in case.

"Come on, Chey-Chey."

She runs to me. I take her by the hand and we walk out into the cool California evening.

"I knew we'd get hired. I knew we would," Jerry says, "but then I started thinking about how my face looked that day, and I got worried."

"I was afraid to count on it," I say.

"Not a good attitude," Jerry says with a smile. "My mom always says if you expect good things they're a lot more likely to come your way."

I think about that. How my mom was so afraid of losing more love after Benson died, she set herself up to live without it.

We stand by the lake for a while, watching the same boy fish that Cheyenne watched last week. He smiles a shy smile at us, but when we say "hi" he doesn't answer. I think maybe he doesn't speak English.

"Let's go over by the slides," Jerry says.

We sit in the sand while Cheyenne climbs up to the top of the slide and then comes whisking down, over and over.

"Our first real job," Jerry says. "It's like we're adults . . . Well, I guess you're already an adult, being a mom and all."

"Yeah, but the job's a big deal to me, too," I tell him. "But it's more complicated for me."

"How?"

"Well, transportation's easier for you, because you've got a car. And the big thing for me is finding a good day care situation for Cheyenne. Except for those few weeks when we were out in the desert, I've never left her anywhere but the Hamilton

Infant Center."

"Couldn't you still do that?"

"I wish. But they only take the children of students attending that school district."

"What about your mom?"

"It would be too much for her, and I think Cheyenne would get bored. She really likes being around other little kids. Every morning now she wants the school van to pick us up."

"And there's this 'proper business attire' thing, too. You just have to have a couple of white shirts, one to wash and one to wear, and the same with dark pants, and five different ties, and you're set. I should have five distinctly different outfits."

"So what are you going to do?" Jerry says.

"Work it out," I say, hoping I can.

I decide to go back to Hamilton High for the last three days. I can take my finals then and go to the Peer Counseling party. That's the kind of final Woodsie gives, a party.

Cheyenne is so excited to see Ethan and Brittany at the Infant Center that she runs around in circles until she's dizzy.

"Welcome back," Bergie laughs. "And how are things going for you, Melissa?"

"Good. Really good," I tell her.

"No more problems with Rudy?"

"No. But he doesn't know where I live . . . Has he been around here?"

"Not since the restraining order. I've not seen a thing of his mother, either. But did you notice what we got since the last time you were here?"

"The fence?" I say.

"Yep. Eight feet tall. Makes the place look like a prison, but no one gets through the gate now without proper ID. I've been asking for better security here for years. It took your Rudy to get it for us," she laughs.

"Not *my* Rudy," I say.

"Good," she says.

On the courtyard people are passing around yearbooks for signing, saying how much they'll miss each other and talking about summer plans. Josh from Peer Counseling asks me to sign his.

"I wish I had one for you to sign," I tell him. "I didn't order one in time."

This is not exactly a lie. I *didn't* order one, but it was because I couldn't afford it. Maybe, if I do well on my new job, Cheyenne won't ever have to worry about not being able to afford scout uniforms, or drill team outfits, or yearbooks.

I write the only thing I can think of to write, "Dear Josh, I enjoyed being in Peer Counseling with you. Good luck in the future. Your friend, Melissa Fisher."

I hand back his yearbook and go looking for Leticia. There is some kind of commotion over by the gate. Rudy? But it's just some kids joking around with the security guard. I'm jumpy, I guess.

In Peer Counseling we eat pizza and sit around talking. Woodsie comes over and sits next to me and Leticia.

"What are your plans for next year?" she asks.

"Cal State Fullerton — track scholarship," Leticia says.

"Wonderful! What major?"

"Probably P.E. I'm not sure yet."

"How about you, Melissa?"

I tell her about my job.

"Good for you," she says. "But keep learning. Maybe take a college night class now and then. You're very smart, you know."

I nod. Maybe I will do that someday. Right now, it seems like if I can take good care of Cheyenne and work full-time, that's a lot. I wonder if Woodsie has kids.

I'm sorry to miss graduation, but if Rudy were to come looking for me anywhere, that would be the place. He knows how
much I wanted to graduate up there with my class. The important thing though, is that I've done all the work, I've finished
with good grades, and the diploma is mine. I just have to wait
for it to come in the mail instead of getting it on stage.

Mom and Teresa are going to take me out to dinner graduation night, and then Teresa's going to keep Cheyenne while me
and Mom go to a movie. It's not cap and gown on stage and then
Grad Nite at Disneyland, but it's not a kick in the shin, either.

20

J OURNAL ENTRY, 3:15 a.m., Saturday night, Sunday morning, I mean.

I can't believe how long it's been since I've written anything here — before school was out, a little over two months ago. Yikes. A lot has changed since then, except that I still write in the bathroom, sitting on the closed toilet seat lid, so the light won't disturb anyone.

Teresa and Mom and I are looking for a three bedroom place, something with a little yard, because it's just too crowded here. Teresa doesn't complain, but I know she's tired of sleeping on the couch. Now that I'm working I can pay my full share of the rent, so we should be able to find something.

Anyway, I want to get caught up with what's been happening, and then for sure I'll write at least once a week. Maybe it's okay that I haven't written lately — maybe I'm not as unhappy or confused as when I was writing a lot.

Well, here goes.

At first I thought I'd never learn all I needed to know to do a good job at Graphic Design Services. There were times I expected my boss, Ms. Lopez, to fire me on the spot. Like when I thought I'd messed up the whole computer program so no one could get paid on time. But then she came to my desk and helped me work through it, step by step. Now, after being there almost two months, payroll is easy for me and it always goes out on time. I'm learning to do quarterly reports, too.

I still like the fact that my computer behaves the same way day after day. Also, I like coming in at the same time each day, and saying hello to the same people, and leaving at the same time. It feels safe to me.

I *love* getting a paycheck. It was a shock to me at first to see that out of $560.00 for two weeks I only got to keep $445.27. So now I'm paying taxes rather than taking money from other people's taxes. That's fair. I want to pay my own way. I hope I never ever have to sit in that welfare office again. I'm pretty sure I won't.

Right off the top of each paycheck, I give my mom and Teresa $170 for my share of rent and food. Then another $240 goes to the day care center. The rest goes for clothes and diapers for Cheyenne, and replacing some of the necessary items that got left behind at Rudy's. Last month I bought her a carseat and this month I'll try to find a used high chair at a yard sale or thrift store. Then, I need clothes for me, too. Slowly I'm trying to get things to wear to work. There's a limit to how many days a week I can wear the black skirt and pink T-shirt without being embarrassed about it. Jerry says no one notices, but I notice.

Speaking of Jerry, he has a desk two cubicles down from me, and he was right when he first predicted we'd be seeing each other at the water cooler. We usually eat lunch together, too, and he takes me to the Metrolink stop in the evenings after work. It's right on his way home. He picks me up there in the mornings, too. A lot of people at work think Jerry and I are together, but it's not like that at all. We're just friends.

Here's how some things are different for us, though. Jerry is getting a brand new car next month. He can easily afford car payments. He doesn't have to pay a big day care hunk from each paycheck, and he doesn't give his mom rent money because he still helps in her Amway business.

It's hard working full time and being the kind of mom I want to be for Cheyenne. I don't get to see her during the day as much as I did when I was at Hamilton High and she was at the Infant Center. For one thing, I wasn't in classes forty hours a week, like I'm at work forty hours a week now. And for another, when I spent time as an aide at the Infant Center, I got to see her there, too. I'm still the first one she sees in the morning, and the last one she sees at night, though. And, truthfully, I think I miss her more than she misses me.

She loves the new day care place. It's at a church near where we live. We walk there early each morning, and from there I walk to the Metrolink stop.

As soon as we open the door at the Play Factory, she yells "bye," and runs straight to the animals. They've got rabbits, turtles, and hamsters, and she checks right away to be sure they all have food and water.

Once a week the kids have a cooking day. They cook real food, not pretend food. Yesterday when I picked her up she gave me a cookie that she'd made herself.

"They like to put a lot of effort into working and reworking the dough," her teacher said, smiling as she watched me bite down hard on the tough little cookie. "We use molasses because it doesn't show the dirt so much."

"Yum," I said.

It's funny, Cheyenne hardly ever mentions Rudy or Irma anymore, not like when we went to the shelter in the desert and she'd say how she missed them, or she'd think she saw one of them and take off running, yelling "Daddy, Daddy," or "Gramma." Now when she sees a guy who looks a little like

Rudy she gets all worried and says, "Daddy 'care me." And I say, "Yes, Daddy can be scary sometimes, can't he?"

I've made up my mind I'm not going to lie to her. When she's older, and starts asking questions, I'll tell her the truth, straight out. None of this "That's water under the bridge" stuff.

And . . . speaking of water under the bridge, my mom hasn't used that phrase once since the day of our picnic. She even dug out a box of pictures that she'd been keeping on her closet shelf. The string that held it together was so old it crumbled to pieces when she untied it.

"You might like to see these," she said, handing me the box.

There was a wedding picture of my grandparents which I studied for a long time, trying to find some resemblance. I think maybe Cheyenne looks a little bit like her great-grandmother, but I can't be sure.

There was a snapshot of Mom and Benson all dressed up. And lots of baby pictures of me. Nothing after I was four, though. And no pictures of any of my possible fathers.

It's hard for me to explain, but seeing even those few pictures and hearing a little more about my early years helps me feel more connected in the world, or like I have more substance. I know that doesn't exactly make sense, but somehow it's important to me to see the pictures and hear the stories. I want to take plenty of pictures, so Cheyenne will know a lot about her life.

The chemo stuff is bad. Mom's hair is coming out in big globs now, and she's lost a lot of weight. Sometimes, when Cheyenne and I get home in the evenings, Mom's in bed with a bucket beside her. She can't even get to the bathroom to throw up, and right after chemotherapy she has to throw up all the time. I try to help out when things are bad for her, clean up after her, sponge her face with cool water, bring her diluted lemonade to take the nasty taste from her mouth. It's awful to see her like that.

"Gramma June sick," Cheyenne says, pulling her mouth

down, when she sees Mom in bed with the bucket beside her.

Then, a few days later, when the effects of chemo have worn off, Mom's bustling around like any other healthy person.

When Cheyenne sees that, she says, "Gramma June better," flashing a big smile at Mom and holding her arms out to her. Mom picks Cheyenne up and smothers her with kisses.

I don't know how it's going to end up. Some days I think my mom could die any minute, and other days I think she could go on forever. The doctors say her "cancer indicators" are down, but I'm not sure what that means in real life.

I'm really sorry she got cancer, and I hope this doesn't sound too selfish, but I'm glad *something* made her review her life. I've had more of a mom these past few months than any other time I can remember. I know that's important to her, too. I can tell.

It's amazing to me, when I think about it, all the changes in my life just during the past six months. I love working at Graphic Design Services, having a *real* job and having the independence a paycheck can bring. And I love being able to talk with my mom, and learn more about my past. And God, how I love having friends, and being able to talk with them on the phone, or go to the park with them, or have them drop by to see me. All the time I was with Rudy, he'd go nuts if anyone called. I wasn't supposed to talk to anyone but him — he was even jealous of girls. The strange thing is, I didn't know how much I was missing. All I was doing was trying not to get Rudy mad. That's no kind of life.

Now, coming home in the evening, walking hand in hand with Cheyenne, I know Teresa will be happy to see us, and Mom, too, if she's up. It's easy to walk into our apartment. Anger doesn't hang from the ceiling and lurk in the corners, waiting to pounce.

At first, when I started at Graphic Design Services, I thought I might just always work there — someday be a supervisor, make a little more money year by year. But I'm not so sure now. As much as I like the safe predictability of it all, I notice that people who've been there for five or six years have really boring conversations in the lounge.

I keep thinking about what Woodsie said, that I should take evening college classes. I might do that in the spring. First I've got to get used to this new life. And I don't want to take any more time away from Cheyenne. But I'll keep the college idea tucked away for later. Right now, I've got my hands full. It's a good full, though. It's not hands full of meanness and trouble.

There are some things . . .

In the middle of the night, when my brain is asleep, my heart still reaches for Rudy. I turn to his side of the bed and the emptiness there floods through me. Then I've got to get my brain awake, remember the words, bitch, whore, slut, remember the killing force of the narrowly missed magazine rack, the raw shin, the bruised face, the scared baby. Then the emptiness fills with anticipation of seeing Cheyenne happy, running to the day care animals, of the smooth quiet ride on the Metrolink, the predictability of Jerry and work, the evening at home with pleasant talk, and laughter, and even if we argue, it's not bitch, slut, whore, hit, kick, smash.

Rudy was, after all, my first, my only, love. And even though I understand now that my love for him was totally misguided, and his love for me wasn't love at all but some kind of sick need to own me, there is still a pull that sneaks up on me and frightens me with its force.

When Cheyenne and I walk down the church hallway to the Play Factory, I usually pause at a bulletin board that has fliers about various meetings. They have AA meetings, youth groups, prayer groups, English classes, study groups, basketball, all kinds of things. Yesterday I saw a flier for a support group for victims of domestic violence. I don't think of myself as a victim, but sometimes, for no apparent reason, I get all shaky. It starts with an inside fluttery feeling, and then my hands sweat, and sweat pours off my face and I tremble all over.

If I get one of those spells at work, I have to put my head down on my desk and do the deep cleansing breath thing, just to get steady enough that I can walk to the rest room. Once I had to lie down on the cot in there for about ten minutes before I could go back to work.

Ms. Lopez noticed and wanted to know what was wrong. I told her I didn't know. That's the truth. I don't know what's wrong. But I think it may have to do with all I've been through with Rudy.

I'm worried, too, about Rudy's hearing. No date's been set yet, but it'll probably be pretty soon. I'll have to go to that, and testify. I really don't want to see him, or Irma, but there's no way out of it.

And, speaking of Irma, I'm pretty sure she has no idea where we live, or where Cheyenne goes to day care, but her threats still hang over my head. I hope she's given up any ideas about getting Cheyenne, but I have an uneasy feeling about her.

Besides all the Rudy/Irma mess, I still have such a heavy sadness for Daphne that sometimes it's like a physical pain in my chest. I guess you could say my life's not perfect, but it's sure a lot better than it was a few months ago.

I know Peer Counseling and the group meetings at the shelter really helped me figure some things out. Writing here in my journal helps, too. But maybe I need other people to talk with about some feelings I still don't understand — people who've been through some of the same stuff. So I suppose the group that meets at the church might help.

Now, the increasing sounds of traffic outside the apartment tell me that morning is about to begin. My butt is numb from sitting here so long. *I will not let more than a week pass before writing again. I will not let more than a week pass before writing again.* I should make myself write that one hundred times, but I hear noises in the kitchen that probably need my attention.

"**C**heyenne!" I whisper, trying not to wake Mom or Teresa.

She has pushed the kitchen table over to the counter, climbed from that to the top of the counter, and is perched on the very edge, trying to reach the cereal on the top cupboard shelf.

I walk quickly to her and pick her up.

"Cheyenne help! Cheyenne help!" she cries, pounding my chest.

"Okay, okay," I say, laughing. "But I don't want you to fall."

"Cheyenne help!"

I lift her high, but she can't quite reach the cereal. I pull a stool over to the counter, stand on it, and then she can reach the box of Cheerios. I put her down. She carries the Cheerios to the table, goes to the refrigerator for milk, and carries that to the table. She gets a bowl from the lower cupboard and a spoon from the drawer, straightens the telephone books on her chair and climbs on top. She dumps too much cereal in her bowl, carefully pours milk on top, picks up her spoon and takes a giant bite.

"Cheyenne help!" she says, beaming at me, milk running down her chin.

"I know, you're not a baby anymore, are you?"

"No baby help! Cheyenne help!"

"You make me laugh," I tell her.

I pour us both some orange juice and check the time. I'm anxious to get ready for work this morning because finally I've got something new to wear. It's a lime green skirt with a green and white top. It's from the everything under $9.00 store. And I've got the white sandals from last payday.

"Morning," Teresa calls from the couch turned bed.

"Are you fully awake?" I call back.

She laughs. "Fully awake is right. 'Cheyenne help,'" she quotes.

"Come on, then, Chey-Chey. We'll take your breakfast in to the coffee table and you can watch 'Sesame Street' with Teresa while Mommy takes her shower. Okay?"

"Okay," they both say at once.

I get Cheyenne set up, then quick grab my stuff and head for the bathroom. When I come back out I parade myself in front of them to show off my new outfit.

"Wow!" Cheyenne says.

"Very nice," Teresa says, then goes to take her turn in the shower.

I bring Cheyenne's clothes out and change her while the count identifies numbers as they flash across the screen. There's Big Bird, and Elmo, and Bert and Ernie, and Prairie Dawn, and they don't all have to have dads, or moms even, to get along in the world. "Sunny day, sweepin' the clouds away, on our way to where the air is sweet . . . " Cheyenne and I sing along.

So many people have helped us move from an awful spot to a pretty good one — Bergie and Woodsie and the hotline people who first got me thinking about the mess I was in. And Carla and Vicky and Daphne and all the others at the shelter. And Mr. Raley — if it wasn't for him I wouldn't have my job. And Leticia, and my mom and Teresa. Jerry, too. And Sean.

I think about what Bergie said, that she hoped I was getting all of my bad luck out of the way during the first nineteen years of my life, and I remember how I always used to think my thirteen letter name was a bad luck name. But it's not so much luck that makes life what it is, it's choices, and people helping one another, and learning to lean toward the good.

"Here," I say, handing Cheyenne the rolled up, smelly, urine soaked diaper from last night.

She throws it into the trash, gets the stool, drags it up to the sink and reaches for the soap. I hand it to her. She hands it back.

"Cheyenne help!" she says, like how many times do I have to tell you that, Mom?

I put the soap back, she stands on the stool on tippy-toes, reaches it, turns on the water and scrubs her hands.

"Cheyenne help," she smiles.

"Backpack time," I say.

She stuffs Mary and extra diapers into her pack and slips it over her shoulders.

"Bye, Teresa!" she yells outside the bathroom door.

"Bye, Sweetie," Teresa yells back.

She walks softly into Mom's room. Mom opens her eyes and smiles.

"Bye, Gramma June," Cheyenne says, running to her and kissing her bald head.

"Good luck with the tests today, Mom," I say, knowing if these tests turn out well she can let up on the chemotherapy for a while.

"Thanks," she says. "Thank you both."

On our way to the Play Factory, morning light reflects brightly from the lake at the park.

"Look, Cheyenne, see how the sun shines off the water?"

"Sunny day, sweepin' the clouds away . . . " she starts singing, and I join in.

Of all the help we've had, it was baby help, and now Cheyenne help, that keeps me moving toward where the air is sweet.

ABOUT

THE

AUTHOR

In addition to **Baby Help,** Marilyn Reynolds is the author of four other young adult novels, **But What About Me?, Too Soon for Jeff, Detour for Emmy,** and **Telling,** and a book of short stories, **Beyond Dreams,** all part of the popular **True-to-Life Series from Hamilton High.**

School Library Journal said of **But What About Me?,** "The writing is superb and the realistic tone sets this book alongside the best of the genre."

According to *Booklist,* **Too Soon for Jeff** *is* a teen father's story which is "a thoughtful book for both young men and young women." This novel was adapted for an ABC After-School Special aired September, 1996, and was nominated for two Emmy awards.

Detour for Emmy, a teen mother's story which *Kliatt* described as "honest, heart-wrenching, inspirational, informative," won the 1995-1996 South Carolina Young Adult Book Award.

Reviewing the short stories in **Beyond Dreams,** *Booklist* states, "All the young people are believable, likeable, and appropriately thoughtful . . . the stories are interesting and well paced . . . "

Of *Telling,* a story in which twelve-year-old Cassie is being molested by a neighbor, *School Library Journal* states, "Reynolds has done a superb job of weaving the complexities of difficult issues into the life of an innocent child."

Each of the previous books in this series has been recognized by the American Library Association, either on their Best Books for Young Adults list, or as a Best Book for Reluctant Readers. All have been selected for the New York Public Library's list of Books for the Teen-Age Reader.

Reynolds continues to work with students at Century High School, Alhambra, California, and to seek their insights on early drafts of her stories. This helps her keep in touch with the realities of today's teens, realities which are readily apparent in her books.

On the home front, Reynolds keeps the bird feeders filled, enjoys visits from her grandchildren, and maintains a demanding exercise/vitamin regimen in a desperate attempt to counteract the ravages of time. She lives in Southern California with her husband, Mike. They are the parents of three grown children, Sharon, Cindi, and Matt, and the grandparents of Ashley, Kerry, and Subei.

OTHER RESOURCES FROM MORNING GLORY PRESS

Fiction:

DETOUR FOR EMMY. Novel about teenage pregnancy by Reynolds.

TOO SOON FOR JEFF. Novel from teen father's perspective. By Marilyn Reynolds.

TELLING. Novel about sexual molestation of 12-year-old. Reynolds.

BUT WHAT ABOUT ME? Novel by Reynolds — Erica almost loses her own identity as she tries to "save" her boyfriend.

BEYOND DREAMS. Reynolds — Six short stories about teens as they face various crises.

DID MY FIRST MOTHER LOVE ME? A Story for an Adopted Child by Kathryn Miller. Birthmother shares her reasons for placing her child.

Non-Fiction:

BREAKING FREE FROM PARTNER ABUSE. Guidance for victims of domestic violence.

TEEN MOMS: THE PAIN AND THE PROMISE. Teen mothers share the realities of their lives. Includes relevant research (eerily similar to the teens' stories) and strong action plan. Ideal for anyone concerned with teen pregnancy prevention.

BOOKS, BABIES AND SCHOOL-AGE PARENTS: How to Teach Pregnant and Parenting Teens to Succeed. Guidelines for teachers working with teen parents.

SURVIVING TEEN PREGNANCY: Choices, Dreams, Decisions. For all pregnant teens—help with decisions, moving on toward goals.

SCHOOL-AGE PARENTS: The Challenge of Three-Generation Living. Help for families when teen daughter (or son) has a child.

DO I HAVE A DADDY? A Story About a Single-Parent Child. Picture/story book especially for children with only one parent. Also available in Spanish, *¿Yo tengo papá?*

WILL THE DOLLARS STRETCH? Four short stories about teen parents moving out on their own. Includes check register exercises.

TEENAGE COUPLES—Caring, Commitment and Change: How to Build a Relationship that Lasts. TEENAGE COUPLES— Coping with Reality: Dealing with Money, In-Laws, Babies and Other Details of Daily Life. Help teen couples develop healthy, loving, relationships.

TEENAGE COUPLES—EXPECTATIONS AND REALITY. For professionals, research results of survey of teenage couples.

TEEN DADS: Rights, Responsibilities and Joys. Parenting book for teenage fathers.

Write for complete catalog.

MORNING GLORY PRESS

6595 San Haroldo Way, Buena Park, CA 90620
714/828-1998 — FAX 714/828-2049

Please send me the following: Price   Total

__ *Baby Help*	Paper, ISBN 1-885356-27-7	8.95	_____
__	Cloth, ISBN 1-885356-26-9	15.95	_____
__ *But What About Me?*	Paper, ISBN 1-885356-10-2	8.95	_____
__	Cloth, ISBN 1-885356-11-0	15.95	_____
__ *Beyond Dreams*	Paper, ISBN 1-885356-00-5	8.95	_____
__	Cloth, ISBN 1-885356-01-3	15.95	_____
__ *Too Soon for Jeff*	Paper, ISBN 0-930934-91-1	8.95	_____
__	Cloth, ISBN 0-930934-90-3	15.95	_____
__ *Detour for Emmy*	Paper, ISBN 0-930934-76-8	8.95	_____
__	Cloth, ISBN 0-930934-75-x	15.95	_____
__ *Telling*	Paper, ISBN 1-885356-03-x	8.95	_____
__	Cloth, ISBN 1-885356-04-8	15.95	_____

Teen Moms: The Pain and the Promise

__	Paper, ISBN 1-885356-25-0	14.95	_____
__	Cloth, ISBN 1-885356-24-2	21.95	_____

Books, Babies and School-Age Parents

__	Paper, ISBN 1-885356-22-6	14.95	_____
__	Cloth, ISBN 1-885356-21-8	21.95	_____

Teenage Couples: Expectations and Reality

__	Paper, ISBN 0-930934-98-9	14.95	_____
__	Cloth, ISBN 0-930934-99-7	21.95	_____

Teenage Couples: Caring, Commitment and Change

__	Paper, ISBN 0-930934-93-8	9.95	_____
__	Cloth, ISBN 0-930934-92-x	15.95	_____

Teenage Couples: Coping with Reality

__	Paper, ISBN 0-930934-86-5	9.95	_____
__	Cloth, ISBN 0-930934-87-3	15.95	_____

School-Age Parents: The Challenge

__ *of Three-Gen. Living* Pap. ISBN 0-930934-78-4		10.95	_____
__ *Teen Dads*	Paper, ISBN 0-930934-78-4	9.95	_____
__ *Do I Have a Daddy?*	Cloth, ISBN 0-930934-45-8	12.95	_____
__ *Did My First Mother Love Me?* ISBN 0-930934-85-7		12.95	_____
__ *Breaking Free from Partner Abuse* 0-930934-74-1		7.95	_____
__ *Surviving Teen Pregnancy* Paper, 1-885356-06-4		11.95	_____
__ *Will the Dollars Stretch?* Paper, ISBN 1-885356-12-9		6.95	_____

TOTAL _____

Please add postage: 10% of total—Min., $3.50   _____
California residents add 7.75% sales tax   _____

TOTAL _____

Ask about quantity discounts, Teacher, Student Guides.
Prepayment requested. School/library purchase orders accepted.
If not satisfied, return in 15 days for refund.

NAME _____

ADDRESS _____

_____

PHONE _____